Last Chance Christmas

Last Chance Ranch Book 6

Liz Isaacson

ISBN-13: 978-1638761501

Chapter One

Lance Longcomb bent to get another brick, the wicked January wind threatening to unseat his cowboy hat. He mashed it on his head, actually grateful for it. Laying brick was no joke, and though the weather had threatened rain today, so far, only the sky foamed with angry clouds. No moisture yet.

He'd cover the new entrance gate to the ranch once it did, but it wouldn't be the end of his workday. Lance spent long hours in the Canine Club and out with the horses when he wasn't doing specific tasks Hudson assigned him.

Working kept him busy. Kept his thoughts from going around and around in circles. Kept him from reminding himself that the only woman he'd had eyes for in the past two years had yet another boyfriend.

Not only that, but Amber was dating another cowboy on the ranch. Dave had told Lance to wait. Watch. She'd break up with him eventually. And she had. But before Lance could ask her out, Ames had. That hadn't lasted long. And now she was seeing another volunteer, one who came out to the ranch several times a week.

"Gotta move on," Lance muttered to himself. Problem was, there was nowhere to move to, and no one else he even cared about. So he mixed cement and layered it on top of the row he'd already done. Put the bricks on. Moved the trowel.

Work, work, work.

And when he wasn't working, he spent time with his band, though they'd all now found women to love. Dave and Sawyer and Carson were all married now, and Cache and Karla would be before long.

Lance had honestly started spending more time with Ames, Cook, and Gray, though the cowboy from down south annoyed Lance with his loud voice and general arrogance.

The engine of a truck met his ears, and Lance stood back off the road as Dave's big black truck rumbled by. He pulled to a stop next to Lance, who said, "Going to the base?"

"Yep." Dave looked at him and then the wall. "What are you doin' this weekend?"

"Same old," Lance said. And he was tired of it. Something in his life had to change, but he didn't know what. *Show me what to do, Lord,* he thought as Dave knocked on the side of his truck.

"See you Monday."

"Have a good one." Lance lifted one gloved hand in good-bye, wishing he was the one driving away from the ranch.

Even as he thought it, he knew it wasn't true. Last Chance Ranch had been a sanctuary to him the same way it was for the rescue animals so many labored to help and protect. He'd come to the ranch after the death of his father that had left his heart broken and his soul filled with darkness.

With prayer and the new job, he'd managed to keep getting up in the morning. With the help of his family and his new cowboy friends, he'd managed to find a measure of joy again. He still felt somewhat empty inside, though every time he went to church, that lessened.

At least until he saw Amber again.

Then he was reminded of his insane attraction to her. Sure, she was beautiful, with long, gorgeous blonde hair Lance wanted nothing more than to fist in his fingers as he kissed her. But he'd been around pretty women before. Lots of them. He'd married one.

Why Amber affected him so strongly, he wasn't sure. Only that something had sparked the moment he'd laid eyes on her and hadn't stopped in the time they'd worked together, despite him going out with other women. Despite her flitting from one boyfriend to the next every few months.

He'd love to be with her for just a few months.

Thunder clapped in the clouds above, and Lance decided he'd set his last brick for the day. He hurried to pull the thick plastic over the section of the wall he'd been working on for a couple of hours. No reason to have to redo it later, and he really liked the red brick Hudson and Scarlett had chosen for the gate flanking the dirt road up to the ranch.

They still had Prime, the robot mailbox that welcomed everyone to the ranch once they'd gone a half a mile down that dirt road. The wreath and tinsel that Prime had been holding for a month was gone now, and soon he'd have a big pink heart on his chest to celebrate Valentine's Day.

Lance was dreading the holiday, but he put it out of his mind as he stepped into the road, tugging on the plastic to get it into place.

A car turned off the main road at a speed that was much too fast for him to get out of the way. He froze, the same way deer did, he supposed.

The driver slammed on the brakes, and Lance managed to dance out of the way. The car swerved toward the wall he'd spent the last three hours building, and he thought that might be as bad as him getting hit by the vehicle.

"Wait, wait," he said as the car came to a stop. Frustration and annoyance surged within him, but he just stood there with one hand clutching the plastic that still wasn't in place. His heart pounded in his chest as the first raindrops fell.

The driver's door opened, and a woman jumped from the car. Not just any woman. Amber Haws.

"Lance," she said, her voice high-pitched, her face red, her eyes weeping. "I'm so sorry." She sobbed immediately afterward, and Lance had no idea what to do.

He looked at the wall, which she hadn't touched. With his eyes back on her, he had no idea what to do. "You didn't hit it," he said. She had a good three feet to go. He wondered if she'd have hit him, standing in the road.

She shook her head, angry little bursts of movement. The rain started to fall in earnest, and Lance was torn. He needed to cover the wall, but he had the woman of his dreams standing in front of him, crying.

"Amber," he said. "Get in the car, okay? Let me cover up this wall, and I'll come help you."

Thankfully, she did as he said, and he hastened to get the plastic in place. Facing the car, with his shoulders soaking wet, he started toward the passenger door. He opened it and slid in, a sigh slipping between his lips.

Her car smelled like his fantasies. Something floral, something peachy, and something so feminine the hole inside him widened, reminding him of how lonely he was.

"What's going on?" he asked easily, like maybe they'd go to lunch in a few minutes, and they were just catching up on small talk.

"What is with you cowboys?" she asked, her voice full of acid. She looked at him, the brown eyes that often followed him into sleep accusatory and full of sharpness.

"I'm sorry?"

"I'm so done with cowboys. Just done." She clenched her fingers around the steering wheel. "Rude, ignorant, arrogant...." Her voice trailed off as she put her car in reverse and got it centered back on the road.

Lance had no idea what was going on, but he knew he didn't need a ride up to the ranch. "Hey, I have my truck," he said as she jammed her foot on the accelerator. He grunted and reached for the handle above the window as he got whiplashed backward.

Amber slammed on the brakes again, and Lance severely regretted getting in the car with her. He thought maybe he'd be able to help her, make her see that all that flirting six months ago had been real for him. That he wanted to touch her softly again, laugh with her, show her that not all cowboys were bad.

She skidded to a stop on the road beside where he'd left his truck. "There you go."

His chest heaved as if he'd just run a marathon, and adrenaline skipped through his bloodstream. He looked at her, the fire in her face scorching hot. "Amber," he said, but he didn't know how to finish it.

"Dwayne broke up with me," she said, the anger crumpling from her fine features. "On the *phone*, Lance. As he left town." Her breath hitched, and her voice broke, and those fingers strangled the steering wheel.

"I'm sorry," Lance said, though he secretly started

rejoicing. If only she hadn't said *I'm so done with cowboys. Just done.*

As far as he'd known, Dwayne wasn't even a cowboy. Sure, he might wear a hat when he came out to walk dogs, but that didn't make him a cowboy.

"I don't mean to be rude," she said. "But I'm late for work."

Time spun forward then, and Lance scrambled for the door handle. "Of course. I'm—I'll—sorry." He got out of the car and backed up as she floored the accelerator again. The tires spun on the slightly wet dirt, and when they found purchase, they kicked gravel out behind them.

Lance stood there as the sky opened up and drenched him, sure the woman had just driven away with his heart.

WHEN HIS DOORBELL rang that night, Lance just glanced at it. It could only be one of three people, and Cache, Ames, Cook, or Gray would just walk in. Sure enough, the door opened a moment later, and Cache walked in, a couple of pizza boxes in his hand.

Ames and Cook entered behind him, and while Lance was happy for the food, he didn't really want the company. He'd been going over everything he and Amber had said to each other last July when they'd flirted at the animal adoption event.

That had been a great few hours and then a few days.

But she'd started dating someone else, and Lance had faded into the background again.

But she had to know how much he liked her. Maybe he should ask her out now. Not wait another moment. Another hour. Another day.

Sure, she'd almost hit him and then the wall he'd been building. She'd been crying and had basically sworn off men right in front of him. But someone else would ask her out, and she'd say yes. Lance just knew it.

Lance wanted to be the guy she said yes to.

"Supreme and Hawaiian," Cache said. "Karla's bringing dessert, if that's all right."

"I don't mean to keep you from her," Lance said, pushing himself off the couch. His whole body hurt, but he didn't let the groan come out of his mouth.

"She said she'd give us a twenty-minute head start," Cache said, moving into the kitchen and putting the pizza on the counter.

"Head start for what?" Lance asked.

"All the women have been with Amber all afternoon." Cache faced him, his eyes bright and shining and knowing. "Her boyfriend broke up with her. Now's your chance, man."

Lance opened his mouth to respond, but no words came. He scoffed and looked at Ames and then Cook. "What's he talking about?"

"You're not going to let her get away again," Cook said. "We're not going to let you."

"Yeah," Cache said. "So we have twenty minutes to figure out your next move with Amber, or else Karla's going to tell you what to do."

Horror struck Lance right between the ribs. "I don't need all the women on this ranch gossiping about me," he said.

"It's not *all* the women," Cache said. "Just Karla, and only because I may have mentioned something about you and Amber."

"Cache," Lance said, exasperated with everything lately. He got out a stack of paper plates and opened the pizza boxes.

"Okay, here's what you're going to do," Cache said, a huge smile on his face. "And just listen all the way to the end."

Lance felt his hopes crash back to the ground with those words, but at least he could eat while his friends talked.

Chapter Two

Amber Haws woke on Saturday morning to the scent of hand sanitizer. The entire volunteer building smelled like it, as everyone had to clean their hands constantly. They used it when they entered the house to sign in. When they left. In every enclosure they went inside.

Honestly, the antiseptic scent turned her stomach.

As did the fact that she'd slept in the back room of the volunteer house in the first place. But she hadn't been able to face the twenty-minute drive back to her house. Alone. She was so tired of being alone.

Scratch that. She hadn't spent much time alone in the past couple of years. There were no shortage of men willing to ask her out, and Amber didn't have a problem saying yes. But she couldn't trust herself anymore.

She always picked the wrong guys to fall for. Dwayne had seemed so normal. So nice. So good.

"Fool," she muttered to herself.

She'd told her friends yesterday afternoon that she was done with dating, and Adele had told her to just give it some time. That she'd find the right man. If that was true, Amber couldn't see it.

She sat up with a sigh and ran both hands down her face. Exhaustion pulled through her, and she wanted a hot shower and a fresh doughnut. A dozen of them. In fact, all she wanted to eat today was doughnuts.

Normally, she didn't work weekends, but she'd putter around up at the ranch today, only so she wouldn't have to face her friends down in town and tell them about Dwayne. Detailing it for the women here at the ranch had been bad enough.

Regret lanced through her. She shouldn't have said anything to Scarlett. But she hadn't been able to work either, and she'd needed someone to help her check-out all the afternoon and evening volunteers. After all, she couldn't do it with tears streaming down her face and inexplicable anger rushing through her every time she saw a cowboy hat come through the door.

Or get in her car.

Double humiliation choked her at how she'd treated Lance Longcomb yesterday. He'd always been nothing but kind and thoughtful with her, and she wondered why he'd never asked her out.

They'd flirted shamelessly six months ago, but he'd never asked. Never said anything. She wasn't sure why. She thought she'd given him plenty of hints that she was interested in him.

Her phone buzzed, and she checked it to find Scarlett had texted. *Someone brought you breakfast this morning. Are you at the volunteer house already?*

Amber didn't want to tell her that she hadn't left. So she simply typed out, *Yep.*

She knew who breakfast was from—Scarlett herself. Well, probably Adele, though she only had a month left of her pregnancy and shouldn't be on her feet at all. But she was exceptionally skilled in the kitchen, and Amber's mouth watered just thinking about the stuffed French toast the woman made.

Amber hoped it was that. With bacon. A lot of bacon. *Candied* bacon.

And since she'd known Adele for a while now, Amber felt certain the woman would know about Amber's obsession with bacon.

You want me to bring it to you? Or do you want to come to the homestead?

Amber didn't want to re-hash everything. So she called Scarlett and said, "I'll come get it, but I don't want to stay."

"Lance is here. I can send him," Scarlett said.

Amber's heart skipped a beat. "Okay," she said. Then she could at least apologize to him for her behavior yesterday.

"Great," Scarlett said. "He's on his way."

Amber said, "Thanks," and hung up. If she was going to face the handsome cowboy and squeeze the words, "I'm sorry," from her throat, she needed to clean up first. She hobbled into the bathroom and turned on the water. She washed her face and slicked her damp hands through her hair, trying to tame the thick curls into something manageable.

She got them all gathered into a bushy ponytail and looked at her makeup-less face. It would have to do. As would yesterday's clothes. In fact, everything about Amber's life felt like yesterday's.

Used up. Old. Crinkled. Rusty. Dry.

Tears gathered behind her eyes again, but she sucked them back. She would not cry today.

She faced herself in the mirror, her eyes darker than she remembered. "Help me, Lord," she said. "It wasn't Lance's fault Dwayne was a jerk." She took a deep breath, feeling stronger than she had since the break-up phone call yesterday.

Her memory for a couple of hours there wasn't great, but she knew she'd almost run over Lance, and then she'd left him standing in the pouring rain.

As she left the bathroom, the front door of the volunteer house opened, and she came face-to-face with the gorgeous cowboy. Her breath caught in her lungs, as it always had when it came to Lance.

He carried a box of doughnuts, and surprise touched

her heart.

"Good morning, Amber," he said, finally coming all the way inside and letting the door close behind him.

"Morning," she croaked. Clearing her throat, she added, "I'm sorry about yesterday."

He waved one hand like what she'd done was no big deal. He was easy-going and laid-back, and she really liked that about him. "It was a rough day for you. I understand." He flashed a smile, the movement in his mouth quick and strong. "I also happen to know you love doughnuts."

He moved over to the counter where the volunteers usually checked in and set the box down. For some reason, Amber couldn't move as she watched him open the box. "Come see."

Their eyes met, and that electric charge that had always existed between them flowed as a live current. It propelled her across the space between them to peer down into the box. An array of chocolate and maple bars sat inside, and she couldn't help giggling.

As the tears came, she spun and grabbed onto Lance. "Thank you," she whispered into his shoulder, thrilled when his arms came around her too, holding her tight, tight against him.

"Listen, Amber." He coughed slightly and continued with, "I know it's not a great time and all that. But I've liked you for a long time, and I'd love to change your mind about cowboys."

Shock and fear made her pull away from him. "Lance—"

"Not right now," he said quickly, his bright blue eyes devouring her. "But I've always waited too long, and then some other guy asks you out. Some idiot like Dwayne." He leaned closer while Amber's mind spun.

I've liked you for a long time.

"So I just wanted you to know. I'm not Dwayne. That guy wasn't even a real cowboy." He took a step back and tipped his hat. "Enjoy your doughnuts." He fell back again, and Amber suddenly didn't want him to leave.

"Stay," she blurted. "I certainly can't eat all of these by myself."

"Yeah?" Lance asked, looking up from under the brim of his hat in the most adorable way.

"Yeah." She smiled and took out a chocolate bar. "Besides, I know you bought these for you anyway. I like the peanut butter ones more than chocolate."

"Oh, sweetheart," he said with a chuckle. "You think I don't know that?" He turned, opened the door, and stuck his hand out. Someone put something in it, and he turned back to her holding another box of doughnuts. He lifted the lid and tilted it toward her, and it only had peanut butter bars in it.

Amber blinked at it, warmth seeping through her, barely covering the surprise and the panic. She couldn't get involved with another man right now.

Could she?

Laughter filled her mouth, and she let it out. Lance laughed with her, and someone out on the porch of the volunteer house handed him a gallon of chocolate milk and a stack of cups, and then he locked the door behind him.

As they sat down behind the desk together to eat, Amber couldn't help looking at him again. He wasn't just a man.

He was the best-looking man she'd ever laid eyes on. The kindest.

And he liked her.

Had for a long time.

So maybe she couldn't get involved with another man right now, but she could certainly start dating a cowboy.

———

By LUNCHTIME, Amber walked through her front door without feeling like the weight of the world rested on her shoulders. She'd had a great couple of hours with Lance that morning, and then he'd left with the words, "Whenever you're ready, Amber," and another adorable duck of his cowboy hat.

A cat yowled, and instant regret hit Amber again. "Cyclops," she said, dropping her purse a step inside the front door. "I'm so sorry." She got busy getting out more cat food, though the feline still had a bit of kibble in her bowl.

She was blind in one eye and declawed, but Cyclops still put off plenty of attitude as she waited for Amber to get the cans of wet cat food open. She paced, the cat equivalent of foot-tapping, and Amber kept apologizing until she put the food in front of the feline.

Cyclops dug into the food, and Amber went back to her purse to get her phone as it started ringing. JJ's name sat on the screen, and Amber swiped on the call. "Heya, sis."

A squeal filled the line, and Amber held the phone away from her ear. She giggled until her sister quieted, and then JJ said, "I just got engaged!"

Amber's heart dropped to the floor and rebounded back to its rightful spot in her chest. "Congratulations," she said, her voice hardly sounding like her own. In two weeks, Amber would turn forty, and that would make JJ six years younger than her.

Of course she had her whole life figured out already. Amber hated the poisonous thoughts in her head, but she didn't know what to do about them.

"Tell me how it happened," she said, hoping she could play the role of a supportive older sister for the next hour. She did wish happiness for her sister. Of course she did.

Cyclops finished eating long before JJ stopped talking, and the cat had apparently forgiven Amber, because she jumped into her lap and sat down.

"And I said yes." JJ sighed blissfully.

"That's so great," Amber said. "I'm happy for you, JJ."

"And you have to come shopping with me," her sister said.

"Of course," Amber said, letting some of the engagement excitement bleed into her. "Of course I will." She made plans with her sister for the following weekend, and when she hung up, she decided there was nothing better to do with her Saturday afternoon than take a nap.

Then she wouldn't have to try to make sense of her feelings. Wouldn't have to try to figure out why she couldn't find someone who wanted to commit to her the way JJ had. The way so many people around her had.

She closed her eyes, and the beautiful sight of Lance's face filled her mind. He'd said he'd be ready when she was, but Amber wondered if she should give herself some time before jumping right back into another relationship.

But that didn't mean she couldn't think of him every time she ate a doughnut.

Chapter Three

L ance kept his head down and his hands busy around the ranch, just like he always did. Since Cache had started the cow cuddling program several months ago, Lance had been reassigned to the Canine Club, as the dogs required more hours per day than Cache had to give. The other cowboy had taken most of the chores Lance had used to do with the pigs and any help Hudson and Dave needed with the horses and llamas.

Not only that, but the large care veterinarian had been training Cache as Gina simply couldn't be everywhere.

Lance didn't mind. He loved dogs almost as much as humans. More, probably, as they did what he said and didn't make him second-guess everything.

He'd done exactly what Ames and Cache had advised him to, and even he could admit that the hour he and Amber had shared eating doughnuts and drinking milk had gone well. She'd filled the volunteer house with smiles and laughter, though she'd looked absolutely broken when he'd first walked in.

A week had passed, though, and she hadn't texted him. Hadn't said more than a couple of words to him when their paths crossed between the Goat Grounds and the Canine Club.

He told himself to be patient. Cache told him to be patient. It felt like the whole ranch was holding its breath, waiting for Amber to make the next move. Lance had obviously bounced a big ball to her, and she'd just had something traumatic happen to her.

He could wait. Heck, he'd been waiting for two years already.

Another week and another Sabbath Day found him on the bench with Dave and Sissy. Lance basked in the contentment and peace that came from his friends. Dave had always been kind to him, and he'd offered a fair share of advice about Amber over the months as well. He hadn't been part of the intervention a couple of weeks ago, and Lance wondered what he'd say now.

A sigh slipped from his lips before he even realized it, and Sissy looked at him. He gave her a quick smile and focused back on Pastor Williams. But his attention simply wasn't on the sermon today.

Sissy must be able to communicate with Dave telepathically, because Lance's phone brightened a moment later, buzzing against his thigh. He glanced at it to find his friend's name there and a quick message.

You okay?

Fine, he typed quickly without looking at the man sitting right next to him. *I'm headed out.* He didn't wait for the text to go through. He stood up and walked down the aisle, feeling like every eye had landed on him.

But he couldn't be caged by walls today. After a quick trip to his cabin to change and grab leashes for Ribbon and Maddie, his two rescue dogs, he loaded everything in the back of his truck and said, "Let's go see Rufus."

Forty minutes later, he pulled into his parents' driveway and looked at the two-story white house with blue shutters. He wouldn't necessarily talk about Amber today, but he did like coming to visit his mother.

The simple way his parents had lived reminded him that life didn't need to be complicated. He'd grown up right here in this house, and memories streamed through his mind of the mischief he and his older brother and his younger sister used to get into.

He'd said good-bye to his father right here in this house too, and he'd held his mother's hand while his dad took his last breath. Sudden sadness came over him, but it only stayed for a moment. His father had been old and in so much pain. His death was a mercy Lance had prayed for, though he knew his mother had been lonely this year.

And if there was anything Lance understood, it was loneliness.

He finally got out of the truck, his emotions ping-ponging all over the place today. The booming bark of Rufus could be heard from somewhere in the backyard, and pride dashed through Lance that his pups had stayed in the back of the truck.

Maddie whined, as the little dog still had some fear around bigger dogs. And Rufus was a huge Great Dane mix that didn't know his own size. Ribbon paced, his tongue hanging out of his mouth and his limp noticeable with every step.

"Sit down guys," he said, holding up his fist. Ribbon complied immediately, but Maddie whined and kept her paws up on the tailgate. "Maddie." He lifted his fist as if she couldn't see the sign he'd taught them for sit.

She did, her tail barely touching the metal before he released the tailgate. She leapt from the back with a bark, but Ribbon waited for Lance to pull out the steps so he could get to the ground without jumping.

Then he trotted off toward the side of the house where Maddie had disappeared. Lance didn't worry about them out on the farm, and he grinned at his mother as she came out onto the front porch.

"What are you doing here this early?" she asked with a smile.

He went up the steps saying, "Nothing. Hoping you have something good to eat," and hugged her. Love and relief moved through him at the touch of his mother, and he held her extra-tight, wishing his emotions weren't so close to the surface today.

He wasn't usually an overly emotional guy, but he couldn't seem to let go of his mom either. She held him tight too, as if she could sense she might be the only thing holding him together.

"I'll make coffee," she finally said, and Lance stepped back.

"You feeling okay, Mom?" Lance asked.

His mother shook her head, and Lance saw the exhaustion pinch around her eyes. "I can come another day," he said.

"That's not necessary," she said. "I'll put fresh coffee on, and we can sit on the back porch to keep an eye on your dogs."

"It's Rufus we need to keep an eye on," Lance said as she opened the front door and went inside.

"Right?" She laughed, and Lance joined his chuckle to hers. She set about making coffee while he went outside and let Rufus out of the dog run. He bounded like a deer toward Ribbon and sniffing ensued. At least they'd all stopped barking. Maddie zipped around the yard like a quick bolt of brown lightning, and Lance wished he could experience joy on that level.

He joined his mother on the porch and took the coffee she gave him. "Thanks, Mom." He sighed as he sat, and that caught the attention of his mother. He really needed to figure out how to keep his sighing contained, as Dave had texted three more times since Lance had left the chapel.

"What's new at the ranch?" she asked.

Lance shrugged. "Not much."

"Hmm." She rocked in the chair his father had made for her decades ago, and Lance knew she could outwait him. The woman had the patience of Job, and he wondered if that was where he'd gotten his from too.

Several minutes later, Lance said, "Is everyone coming for lunch today?"

"Not until four."

Same as always. Lane usually joined his family for their Sunday afternoon meal, and he enjoyed his nieces and nephews. No one in his family had ever pressured him to bring anyone, and they didn't ask incessant questions about who he was dating. He'd always been grateful for that, but he found himself wishing someone would ask today.

"Mom, do you think I could ask for some help?"

"Help with what?"

He shifted in his seat and took another sip of his coffee. "A woman I like."

That got her attention, and her blue eyes rounded. "Is it serious?"

"No," he said quickly, refusing to look away from Rufus and Ribbon. "We haven't even gone out. It's... complicated, I guess." But it really wasn't. "I've liked her for a long time, but she always has a boyfriend. Her latest just broke up with her, and I told her I like her. It's been two weeks, and nothing."

He looked at his mother. "Is that normal, or should I accept that she's not interested?" His heart wailed at the very possibility that Amber wouldn't even consider a relationship with him. She'd flirted with him plenty before, and if he hadn't waited, maybe things would've been different.

"Maybe she just needs some time," his mom said. "You've not said anything else?"

"I told her I'd be ready when she was."

"Hmm," his mom said again. Another couple of minutes went by before she said, "Maybe let her know again, Lance."

"How?"

"Most women have a weakness," she said. "Mine was flowers. Whenever your dad wanted to apologize or soften me up to get me to go on a cruise or something, I'd find flowers on the kitchen counter."

Lance enjoyed the stories of his mother and father's marriage, their love for one another. He could hear it in every letter, every word. "I forgot you hate cruises."

"And yet we went on three." She got up, her rocking chair squeaking. "I have to go get the potatoes in the oven."

He nodded, and she left him on the porch with his own thoughts. *Let her know again.*

Find her weakness.

Lance knew a lot about Amber, as they'd been friends

for a couple of years now, and suddenly an idea popped into his mind.

Ballet tickets.

It wasn't even his own thought, and he tipped his head toward the heavens and said, "Thank you, Lord."

THE FOLLOWING EVENING, Lance's throat itched as if he'd swallowed a colony of ants and they were trying to crawl their way back out. Maybe he was coming on too strong. Amber hadn't seemed to have any problems saying yes to other men when they showed interest in her. Maybe she didn't like him. Maybe he'd read all of her signals wrong over the past seven months.

Yet he kept going back to the Fourth of July, when he'd held her hand and they'd flirted shamelessly during the animal adoption event at the church.

What had that been?

He wanted to find out—and he decided if Amber didn't come out and say no, he was going to keep showing her he liked her. With those thoughts in his mind, and the ballet tickets in an envelope in his hand, he went up the steps to the front door of the volunteer house.

Amber had organization down to a science, and Lance had seen the house run without her. Volunteers knew exactly what to do, even if it was their first time out to the rescue ranch. Half of him hoped Amber would be gone for the day already.

She didn't live on the ranch the way most of the cowboys did, and he hadn't bothered to check to see if her car was parked behind the building. The scent of lemons hit him from the candle burning on the check-in desk.

Amber glanced up, her brown eyes brightening when she saw him. That wasn't fake, was it? Would she really look pleased to see him if she wasn't?

"Lance," she said, rising. She smoothed her hands down her pale pink blouse and pressed her lips together. Lance saw every movement, his heart starting to beat faster and faster. He wished this woman didn't have such a great hold over him, but he didn't know what to do about it.

"I'm sorry I haven't called or anything," she said, stepping around the desk. "Things exploded here, and Jewel's been at the ranch with me for a week." She gave him a smile, a bit of trepidation in her eyes.

"It's fine," Lance said, though he thought it wouldn't have been too terribly hard for her to text him and let him know. "I was...It's your birthday today, right?"

She nodded, those brown eyes filled with something he couldn't name, giving him courage to go on.

"Well, happy birthday." He grinned and held up the envelope containing the tickets. "I know you like the ballet, and they're doing Don Quixote this winter. I thought maybe we could go together."

Her eyebrows went up, and she looked from him to the envelope. "The ballet?" She giggled, her eyes positively sparkling now. "I didn't know a big, tough cowboy like you enjoyed the ballet."

Oh, he didn't. But *she* did, and he wanted to be with her. He simply put a smile on his face, and asked, "Is that a yes?" He swallowed, feeling brave as something electric sang along his skin. "The tickets are for Valentine's Day. It's a few weeks away still."

Amber took the envelope from him, but she didn't open it. "Then you should probably take me to dinner this weekend, so we don't have to wait quite so long to see each other again." She looked at the envelope and back to him, that sexy smile stuck to her mouth. "I can't believe you know when my birthday is."

Lance shrugged, because he didn't want to admit he'd been paying such close attention. In a way, he already had. "I'd love to take you to dinner. We can get cake for your birthday."

Chapter Four

Lance was the one bright spot in Amber's life. Training the goats for yoga had become a chore. Color-coding the volunteer packets, which usually made her inner control freak smile, had become boring. Jewel coming into the volunteer house and asking questions, pointing out regulations that Amber had gotten lax on, and various other things had annoyed her.

Yes, she needed to run the volunteer program correctly at Last Chance Ranch. She didn't actually work for the ranch. Her checks came from Forever Friends, and Last Chance Ranch was their biggest rescue sanctuary in the state. They gave the ranch a lot of money, and while it wasn't Amber's job to make sure that was used properly, it was her job to make sure the people taking care of the animals did so properly.

But with Lance standing in front of her, all the stress

of the past week melted away. He'd remembered her birthday, the gesture so sweet and so romantic.

"When do you want to go to dinner?" she asked, taking a step closer. She reached out at the same time she dropped her eyes to his shirt. She fiddled with the button near his throat, that heat between them still there. It had always been there, and she was so glad he'd finally acted on it.

She supposed she could have too, but she'd never had a shortage of men asking her out. None of them had stuck though, and she wondered if anyone ever would.

When he didn't answer, she suggested, "Friday?"

"I have band practice on Friday," he said. "What about tonight?"

Her eyebrows went up again. "Tonight?"

"When are you done here?" He glanced around as if he'd find her to-do list posted for all to see. No, she kept that on various sticky notes behind the desk.

Amber wrestled with herself. She wanted to go out with him, but she wanted more time to prepare. She wanted to experience the excitement and giddiness of waking in the morning with a date with the handsome cowboy on the horizon for that night. She wanted to stand in her closet and choose the exact right outfit. Put on her bright pink lip gloss and hope he'd kiss it off later.

She stalled her thoughts there, because she hadn't even been out with Lance yet. She shouldn't be thinking about kissing him. She shouldn't even be going out with him. Hadn't she sworn off men just a couple of weeks ago?

Go slow, she told herself.

"I can't tonight," she said, though it was her birthday and it would be perfect. "But what about tomorrow?"

"Let me check something." He pulled out his phone and started swiping. Amber opened the envelope and peeked at the tickets. They really were for Valentine's Day, for one of her favorite ballets. She was sure Lance had never been to a ballet before, which made his gesture that much sweeter. None of her other boyfriends had ever taken her to the ballet, though they'd all known she used to dance.

A pang of sadness hit her, stealing her breath for a moment. Startled, she turned away from Lance, who still had his head bent over his phone. It had been many years since she'd put on pointe shoes and taken the stage. Fifteen long years. Why did it still hurt that she'd only had a few years to pursue her dreams? Would it always hurt?

Her phone rang, and she said, "Excuse me," though Lance could obviously keep himself busy for a moment. Her sister's name sat on the screen, and Amber felt the weight of the world settling back onto her shoulders.

"Hey," she answered, thinking JJ just wanted to wish her happy birthday. Neither of her parents had called yet either. "I only have a minute."

"No problem," JJ said. "Mom wants to go shopping

tomorrow night for a few things. Wondered if you wanted to come."

"Tomorrow," Amber said, lifting her eyes to meet Lance's. He nodded, and she said, "Just a sec." She took the phone from her ear. "My sister just got engaged, and she wants to go shopping tomorrow."

"You should go," he said. "I can't tomorrow night anyway. I'm doing a bunch of stuff for Dave so he and Sissy can go see their birth mom."

Amber nodded, knowing Dave and Sissy would be getting a baby as soon as the mother gave birth. She was due the first week of February, and Amber couldn't wait to hold another newborn.

"JJ, I can go tomorrow," she said, her voice filled with defeat her sister wouldn't hear anyway.

"Great, meet at Mom's at six." JJ hung up, sticking true to making the conversation short. Amber set her phone on her desk, feeling done for the day though she still had work to do. Her sister hadn't even mentioned Amber's birthday, which was so like her it hurt. "So Wednesday?" She made her voice as perky as possible to hide the pain cascading through her.

"I can go Wednesday," he said, his gaze locking onto hers.

"Great." Amber smiled even as more words piled up in the back of her throat. "Lance, I—"

He took a step toward her. Then another one. When he stood close enough to touch her, he reached out and tucked her hair behind her ear. "I'm not in a hurry, Amber. I just hadn't heard from you, and I was wondering if I'd overstepped."

"You didn't," she said, her voice sounding as weak as he made her feel. She braced her palm against the desk in front of her.

"Great, so I'll text you before Wednesday. We'll set up a time and all of that. Send me your address. Stuff like that." He cleared his throat, and Amber actually enjoyed that she made him nervous. Lance was so cool. So collected. So calm. So mature. He was unlike any of the other men she'd dated, and he actually made *her* nervous. So it was nice to know she made him a little anxious too.

She nodded.

"Do you have somewhere you like to go?" he asked.

"You choose," she said. "I obviously just like to eat."

He cocked his head, confusion running across his expression. "What does that mean?"

Foolishness hit Amber, and she ducked her head. "I mean, I'm not—I'm not skinny, Lance. It was a joke."

Amber wasn't sure what she was expecting from him, but he edged closer and slipped his arm around her waist. "You're beautiful," he whispered. No sooner had he spoken than he stepped back and headed for the door.

She couldn't keep up with what was going on, but she knew she'd felt incredibly beautiful when he said she was. Heat filled her, only leaving her cold without him nearby.

"Talk to you soon," he said, glancing back at her with that dazzling smile. "Happy birthday."

She nodded, and he left the volunteer house. Amber collapsed into her desk chair, her mind whirring with all that had just happened. Then a slow smile spread across her face.

She had a birthday date with Lance Longcomb to look forward to—and a shopping trip with her mother and sister. The smile slipped a little, but it didn't disappear completely.

"No, Sugar. Get down." Amber pointed to the ground, her fingers pinched around a piece of graham cracker. The baby goat jumped off the block and looked at her, its crazy eyes almost looking in two different directions. She fed the goat her treat.

"You don't go from block to block," she said. "One at a time." The baby goats only weighed about fifteen pounds, but they had hard hooves, and they couldn't hop from person to person during the yoga session. They landed too hard on the second person.

"Try again," she said, moving around the block. She broke off another piece of the cracker and held it up. The baby goat jumped up, and Amber treated her. "Good girl. Down."

The goat got down, and Amber continued directing

her and rewarding her when she did the tasks right. A few minutes later, she put Sugar Baby back in the pasture and said, "All right, Milky Way. Your turn."

This herd of baby goats was brand new, and they hadn't done their first session of yoga with humans yet. It took weeks to train them well enough for them to get in the arena with people, and Amber estimated this group still had a couple of weeks to go before they could start working.

Milky Way was much farther ahead of Sugar Baby, and Amber got down on her hands and knees, and he hopped right up on her back without a verbal cue. She didn't have to treat him right away either.

She lowered her forearms to the ground, and Milky balanced beautifully. She lifted herself again and raised one leg. The goat turned around on her back, but he didn't get down.

She snapped her fingers, and he hopped to the ground, immediately leaping onto the block a few feet from her.

"Good boy," she said, pride moving through her. "You're ready, Milky. Can you get the other babies to shape up?" She grinned at him and fed him several bits of cracker. She'd move him into the yoga sessions this week and see how he did. It would be a good indication of how the others would do as well, and he'd be the center of attention for their yoga instructors.

Still on her knees, she glanced over her shoulder to see if any of the instructors had shown up yet. They had to know all the goats too, and they had to be able to teach a yoga class to forty people while twenty goats ran around, hopping on everyone—the instructors included.

Amber had them come up to the ranch every Tuesday morning for an hour to make sure everyone was ready for the week, and sure enough Diane walked through the gate, a smile on her face.

"Morning," Amber said, getting up and dusting herself off.

"McKenna is right behind me," she said. "Literally. I was in front of her at Brewed." She held out a cup of coffee for Amber, who took it with gratitude.

"Thanks." She smiled at Diane, trying not to let herself slip down the jealousy slope. It was so slippery sometimes, and Diane was tall and lithe and thin, with the perfect skin and miles of dark hair to go with her Hawaiian complexion.

She was also as nice as a person could be, and Amber had gotten along great with her the moment they'd met.

"There's a cowboy down the fence," Diane said, bending to pick up Milky Way. "Looked like he was watching you."

Amber choked on the sip of coffee she'd taken. "Really?" She spun as if she'd see Lance, but she couldn't find anyone standing along the fence.

Diane laughed. "Are you seeing someone again?"

Amber hated the *again* on that question. Really hated it. Her stomach soured, and the coffee tasted nothing but bitter, though she knew there was plenty of sugar in it. "Sort of," she mumbled, wishing McKenna could be on time for once.

"Good for you," Diane said as she got out her yoga mat and started stretching. Milky jumped on her back, and she laughed.

"You think so?" Amber asked, not quite sure why she was unsure about Lance. She wasn't really. She just thought maybe she needed a break from dating. Honestly, getting to know a person and slowly revealing things about herself was exhausting. Texting late at night. Always making sure she looked her best, just in case he stopped by. All of it. Amber was tired of all of it.

"Sure," Diane said. "Why wouldn't you go out with someone else?"

"I don't know," Amber said, shrugging and shying away from the inquisitive look on her friend's face. "I just —I had three boyfriends last year. Moved from one to the next. Don't you ever get tired of it?"

"Honey, I'm married." Diane laughed. "So I'd love to have a date every once in a while."

Amber smiled, and thankfully, McKenna arrived in a whoosh of energy, explanations for why she was late and opening the gate so all the babies could join them in the training arena.

Amber didn't have much time to think about Lance standing down the fence, out of sight, watching her. He lingered nearby in her thoughts, though, and once the training session concluded, she stayed out in the goat barn for a few extra minutes.

With her head bent, she prayed aloud, "Lord, help me know what to do. I've always trusted You, and I know Thou won't lead me astray." She paused, trying to feel something. Trying to hear. Listen.

"Is it me?" she whispered. "What do I need to do to be different? How can I change?" Desperation filled her. Maybe if she'd just been smarter, Corbin wouldn't have broken up with her. Maybe if she'd been thinner, Damien would still be in the picture. Maybe if she'd been more interested in concerts and rodeos, Dwayne wouldn't have left.

Maybe, maybe, maybe.

And maybe none of those men were right for you, her mind whispered.

"Is Lance right for me?" she asked, wanting God to tell her exactly what to do so badly.

He didn't, but Amber finally made her way over to the volunteer house anyway. She didn't know if she needed to change or not. She didn't know if things with Lance would work out or not.

What she did know was that Jewel sat behind the desk when Amber walked in, and she did not look happy. Amber smothered the sigh threatening to come out and said, "I just need to wash my hands. Be right there."

Chapter Five

L ance got the dog-walkers set up with their canines for the morning. He'd awakened that morning with more hope in his heart than he'd had in years. Since his marriage had ended over fifteen years ago, to be precise.

He had no idea where Peggy was now, and he didn't need to know. They'd been married less than year, and they didn't have any kids when she'd declared their marriage "a mistake," and asked him to move out.

He'd been working ranches that came with room and board since, and he'd finally found one where he wanted to stay. It was close enough to his family to not be suffocating, and far enough away to be his own person. Make his own choices.

He hadn't told anyone about the forthcoming date with Amber. Not even Cache, Cook, or Ames. He wasn't sure why not. His date tomorrow night felt like a delicious secret he wanted to keep to himself for a while longer. Maybe forever, if it didn't go well.

He thought about the ballet tickets and how much he'd spent on them. The show wasn't for another month. What if Amber broke up with him before then? He'd seen her dating patterns over the past couple of years. If she didn't like someone, she moved on pretty quickly.

He held onto the electricity that had flowed freely between them in the volunteer house yesterday. That had to mean something.

Lance finished spraying out enclosure three, and he left the doors open so the dogs could go back inside should they want to. They were fed and watered now, and they had water outside as well. Though it was January, it wasn't terribly cold, and most of the dogs liked to spend time outside no matter the temperature.

The radio on his hip buzzed, and a voice said, "Lance, it's Amber. We have a family looking to adopt. Where can I send them to find you?"

His heart ba-bumped in his chest, though this exact message had come over the radio before. She coordinated the adoptions when people showed up at the rescue ranch, but he took people around to meet the dogs they might be interested in.

Most people took a canine home with them for a couple of days before deciding, and the adoption process usually wasn't terribly fast.

"I'll meet them at the gate," Lance said into the radio.

"Great. Five minutes," Amber said, and Lance could've been imagining the smile in her voice. But he didn't think he was. He really needed to stop second-guessing everything. It really wasn't like him, and he'd learned over the years since Peggy had left that he could only deal with problems as they came. No sense in worrying about them before then.

A man and woman arrived at the gate to the Canine Club a few minutes later. They had a little girl with them, probably seven or eight years old, who was in a wheelchair. "Hello," he said, shaking hands with all of them. "Did Amber send you with your dog preferences?"

The girl handed him the pink sheet. As he started looking over it, he asked, "What's your name?"

"Heaven," she said.

Lance glanced up, a smile beaming through him. "That's so pretty. Is this dog for you?"

"Yep," she said. "It's my birthday next week, and my dad said I could get one."

"We want a bigger dog," the dad said, though Lance had already read it on the preference sheet. Amber was nothing if not detailed, and she knew what kind of animal was available, from the pigs to the cats.

"We have a lot of big dogs," Lance said. "It's the little ones that get adopted quickly." He skimmed the sheet again. "You think you might want one you can train?"

"Our daughter has epilepsy," the mother said. "And

43

she suffers from some panic attacks. We've heard dogs can help with both of those."

Lance knew they could, but he felt like he should be honest with them. "They can. But a lot of our dogs here have been traumatized themselves. They're great dogs, don't get me wrong. But they might not be able to do what you want them to." He scanned everyone in the family. "We don't have the popular breeds here, like golden retrievers or German shepherds, or poodles. Those breeds are super smart and easily trained. We have awesome dogs. But it might be a lot of work to do what you want them to do."

"That's okay," the girl said immediately. "Right, Dad?"

The dad wore a pinch of worry in his eyes, but he nodded. "Right."

"I'm sure Amber told you about our overnight trials." Lance turned and started walking toward enclosure two, though the couple of dogs he had in mind might be out in the open area and hard to find. "You can take any dog for a couple of days and see how he or she does in your home. You can bring them back, no questions asked. Adoption doesn't happen until all the paperwork is filled out and payment made."

"She told us," the mom said.

Of course she had. Amber knew how to run the adoption program on the ranch. "Well, I've got a few pups in mind for you. Now we just need to find them." He unlocked the door to enclosure two and held it so the family could enter in front of him. "Oh, look. Apollo is in here. Hey, bud. Come on over."

He stepped over to the third door and said, "This is Apollo. He's a bullmastiff. Part bulldog. Part mastiff." Lance unlocked the door and held out his fist for the dog to sit. "He knows a few things. He'll sit if you hold out your fist like this. And he'll lay down if you point to the ground. He's smart as anything. He came to us from the streets of LA."

With Apollo sitting, Lance stepped back and out of the way. "Come on, bud. Come say hi."

Apollo got up and approached, a smile on his doggy face, but his steps hesitant and slow. The woman crouched down and held out her hand for him to sniff, but he went to the wheelchair first. He licked Heaven's hand first, and she giggled.

Happiness moved through Lance. "He's about five years old. Potty-trained. Crate-trained. Weighs about ninety pounds."

"Oh, he's big," the father said.

"He's big," Lance confirmed, still gazing at Apollo, who had shoved his way between the mom's knees. She patted him, and the dad bent down and did too.

"I like him, Dad," Heaven said.

"Sweetie," her father said. "They have forty-three dogs here. Let's look at more than one, okay?"

Lance flipped over the sheet and stepped over to the door to grab a clipboard. He wrote Apollo's name on the back of the pink paper and grabbed a set of papers that would tell them more about the bullmastiff.

"I've got a Dogue de Bordeaux that's a little smaller. A female. She's in another enclosure, if you want to meet her."

"Yes, let's see a few," the dad said, and Lance put Apollo back in his run and locked the door. While he was glad he had a family here that wanted a rescue dog, he had a feeling this adoption would take a while, and he had double chores to accomplish that day.

At the same time, this adoption meant he had another reason to talk to Amber today. He'd watched her work with her baby goats for a few minutes that morning, and he'd walked away feeling foolish. He had her number. If he wanted contact with her, he could get it without stalking her.

SIX-THIRTY, he confirmed later that night, long after the family had taken Isabella, the Dogue de Bordeax home for the night. Long after he'd finished his and Dave's chores. *Send me your address so I can come pick you up.*

Amber responded a few seconds later with an address down in Pasadena. Lance felt weary to the bone, but he sure did like texting Amber in the darkness of his bedroom.

Did you decide where you wanted to go? He wasn't

sure why she thought she wasn't beautiful. Maybe she had some curves, but it was exactly those that made Lance's mouth water. Or maybe the waves and waves of gently curled hair. Those brown eyes where he'd expected blue.

Surprise me, she said. *I'm so tired. I'll see you tomorrow.*

Lance sent one more text—*Okay*—and clicked off his lamp too. Morning would come early, and he hoped time would continue to pass quickly until his date with Amber that night.

The sun rose, and Lance got to work. Lunchtime came, and he still didn't have a place for dinner that night. He didn't get off the ranch as much as others—as Amber—and he wasn't sure where would be a good place for their first date.

Desperate and in need of help, he finally texted Ames and Cook, both cowboys who seemed to never have a shortage of dates. *Where would be a good dinner place for a first date?*

He wasn't expecting his phone to blow up, but it did, chiming every other second for a good half a minute.

He shook his head as he chuckled, scrolling through the dozen places Ames and Cook had suggested.

Cook's last text made him pause. *Who are you going out with?*

Amber. He typed out the letters and stared at them, the feeling so surreal. Finally. He was going out with Amber Haws, the woman he'd been fixated on for so long.

His fingertips tingled, and he couldn't believe he was only six short hours away from what he hoped would be a good date.

"Please," he whispered to his screen, intending the words to reach God's ears.

He sent the text and didn't bother to put it back on the shelf yet. He expected Cook and Ames to be surprised, and sure enough, a dozen more texts came in. Everything from *About time* to *Congratulations!* to *I'd definitely go with Pages.*

Lance had never heard of Pages, but his phone had the Internet, and he could look it up. Cook had said it was great food with a "low" atmosphere, which Lance didn't understand. But the pictures on his phone painted a better picture for him.

The place looked like it would be romantic, not filled with pounding music or anything that would make it hard to make conversation. The booths were big, and private, and the food looked amazing.

Pages looks great, he sent to his friends. *Thanks.*

Then he did set his phone down and got to work. After all, Hudson and Scarlett weren't paying him to plan his dates.

Lance could barely focus for the rest of the afternoon. Somehow, he got his chores done. Showered. Drove to the appointed address he'd typed into his map app.

He found himself getting out of the truck and walking

toward Amber's front door, the feeling just as surreal now as it had been all day long.

He'd imagined this moment so many times, and his pulse felt like it was trying to spring out of his body. He clutched the bouquet of flowers he didn't remember buying and lifted his hand to ring the doorbell.

It's Amber, he told himself, hoping it would calm him. At the same time, the same words—*it's Amber*—made him feel like throwing up. He'd wanted this date for so long—but what if it turned out badly?

At least his fantasies always ended well. He felt like running away, but before he could move, the sound of the lock twisting met his ears, and he'd never get away without her seeing him now.

Chapter Six

Amber's nerves fluttered in her throat as she took in the glorious sight of Lance on her front steps. He was cowboy perfection, and Amber had always had a weakness for a man in a cowboy hat.

He smiled at her, seemingly perfectly at ease. His strong jaw begged her to touch it, probably moments before she kissed him. Startled she was thinking about kissing already, she only allowed herself a moment to take in the way his shoulders seemed to stretch so wide, that blue and yellow checkered shirt almost like the plaid he wore around the ranch. But more upscale.

He wore jeans and his cowboy boots, but his hat was different tonight too.

"Don't you look great?" he asked, moving the fistful of flowers he held closer to her. "I know you like wildflowers."

She did, and she smiled as she took them. "Thank you." She tipped forward and pressed her lips to his cheek. "You want to come in for a second while I put these in water? Do we have time?"

"Sure," he said. "Got nothing but time."

Amber wasn't the cleanest person on the planet, but she liked things to be in their place. So she knew exactly where her vases were, and she asked him about his mother as she started clipping the stems.

"She's doin' okay." Lance exhaled heavily, which caused Amber to look up.

"Is she?"

"I mean, she seems to be." He shrugged. "I go out there every Sunday. The house isn't falling down, and she has the dog. I think she's just lonely."

Amber nodded, because she understood loneliness. "Understandable." Lance's dad had passed away only a year or so ago, and she knew he missed him too.

"What about your family?" he asked. "JJ is getting married?"

A flash of hurt pressed behind her lungs. "Yes," she managed to say as she poured the flower food into the water. "We went dress shopping yesterday, and wow. She's going to have to postpone the wedding, because she is so particular." She added a light laugh to the statement.

Lance chuckled too, and Amber arranged the wildflowers in the vase and admired them. "They're so beautiful," she murmured.

"Like you," he said, stepping closer to her and slipping his hand into hers. "Are you ready?"

Amber only had to turn her head to look at him. He stood so close, giving off so much warmth and comfort. She just wanted to bask in it for a moment, so she squeezed his hand and leaned her shoulder into his.

"What's wrong?" he asked, his voice quiet and full of compassion.

"Nothing," she said, feeling weak and jealous and stupid about feeling weak and jealous. "Let me grab my purse, and I'll be ready." She put a smile on her face, but it didn't quite sit right.

Lance let her go, but when she faced him again, she saw that edge in his eyes. She'd seen it before around the ranch as they'd worked together. He was a smart man. He might not say everything he was thinking, but he saw things she tried to keep hidden from everyone else.

"Where's Cyclops?" he asked. "And I'm surprised you didn't bring Gemini home with you. You loved the dog."

"I still do," she said. "But she was meant to be with that family." She sighed. "And Cyclops doesn't like visitors. I'm sure she's hiding in my bedroom." She gave Lance a real smile this time. "I'm starving."

"Me too." He took her hand again, but he didn't step toward the door. He pulled her close, slipping his arm around her waist and holding her close. For one breathless moment, she thought he'd kiss her before they even went out.

"We don't have to go," he said, his voice husky. His eyes drifted closed, and he leaned down to press his cheek to hers. "I just—I can tell something's bothering you, and if you don't want to go, that's fine."

She swayed on her feet, and she wasn't sure if it was because of his strength guiding her, or because she'd lost all rational thought at the scent of his cologne, or something else entirely.

But she knew one thing: She wanted to go out with this man. She wanted everyone to see her with him, so they'd know he wasn't available. Not that she'd seen him date much in the time they'd worked together.

"I want to go," she finally said, and he stepped back.

"All right, then. Let's go." He led her to his truck then, and held the door for her while she climbed up. His feelings for her were obvious, and Amber watched him circle the truck to get in, debating on whether she should slide over and sit directly beside him on the seat.

In the end, she didn't. She'd been very forward with her last few boyfriends, and maybe it was time to try something different.

"Have you been to Pages before?" he asked.

"A few times," she said. "It's great."

He fiddled with the radio, turning it down. Amber caught part of the song and said, "I love this one."

She reached over and turned it back up, joy filling her from top to bottom. She belted out the next lyric, determined that her sister's engagement would not cast a dark cloud over her life.

Lance laughed, and Amber decided she didn't care what she'd done on other dates. She slid across the seat, laughing with him. She took his hand in hers and leaned her head against his shoulder.

This was going to be a great date, because she wanted it to be.

THE NEXT DAY, Amber practically floated down the road and up the bluff to the ranch. Her evening with Lance had been fantastic. One of the very best first dates she'd ever been on. "The best," she told herself as she went up the steps to the volunteer house and entered.

"Hey." Lance rose from the chair just inside the door, almost startling her.

"Lance." She carefully stepped all the way inside and closed the door behind her. There had been no kissing last night. He'd walked her to the door and held her tight, said he had the best time, and had turned to go. She'd watched him walk confidently back to his truck, wave to her, and drive off.

"I got a call this morning," he said. "I wanted to talk to you about it real quick before I head over to the Club."

"Sure." She moved past him, somewhat disappointed

he'd been waiting in the house to talk about business. He'd done it before, and they were at work. "What's up?"

"It was the track coach at Farnsworth High. He wondered if we might have some dogs that would like to go running with their students."

Amber put her purse on the desk, lifting her eyes to his. "Really?"

"They're about a mile from the entrance to the ranch," he said. "Coach Tea said he'd have his students run up here, get the dogs, and they could all go for a run together. He thinks it'll motivate some of his students and be good for the dogs."

Amber opened her laptop, though she wasn't going to do anything on it while the gorgeous cowboy stood in front of her. "Do we have dogs that can handle that? It sounds like they might not be on leashes?"

"Oh, they'll have to be on leashes," Lance said. "I can put together a short list of animals that could handle something like this. We have several."

Amber smiled at his enthusiasm. "If you think it's worthwhile, do it."

"Do we have money in the budget to buy vests for them? Something that says 'Adopt me at Last Chance Ranch,' or something like that."

Light filled Amber's soul, and she couldn't help stepping closer to Lance. "That's such a great idea," she said. "I'll talk to Sissy about it today."

"I'll call you later then." He stepped into her personal space, swept his lips across her cheek, and left.

Amber stood there, hardly remembering to breathe or blink, and wondering if this brilliant feeling of being cherished would wear off. Lance almost seemed too good to be true.

What if he was?

SEVERAL DAYS PASSED, and while Lance wasn't in the volunteer house every morning when Amber arrived, as they worked together to put together this new running team of dogs, get vests ordered, and meet with the track coach and his students, Amber did see him more and more.

He didn't ask her out again. He seemed extraordinarily busy around the ranch, which honestly wasn't anything new. There were always five thousand things happening around the ranch, and Lance was a hard worker.

One day near the beginning of February, Amber sat at her desk, on the phone with Jewel's secretary about the paperwork that had been turned in that week, when a bell started ringing.

She jumped to her feet, because when the bell rang at Last Chance Ranch, something big was happening. Could be an amazing thing, or a terrible one. The bell had rung when coyotes had broken some fences, but it had also sounded at all the weddings here at the ranch, and when Jeri and Sawyer had brought home their baby.

Hurrying to wrap up her conversation, she wished she could check her texts. Maybe something had come in. Then she'd know more what to do. The radio on her desk remained silent, so it must not be a life-threatening issue on the ranch.

Which meant something else. No one was getting married, but she knew Scarlett and Hudson were trying to adopt, and Adele was pregnant and due very soon, and Dave and Sissy had a baby coming too. Could she have been born early?

Excitement built in Amber. It had to be Adele, as she'd been on bedrest since Christmas. She dashed out the front door, still talking to Brenda. The volunteer house sat a few hundred yards down the road from the homestead, but the front door faced west. She could see a small crowd had already gathered there, and more people kept arriving.

"I have to call you back," she said as the bell continued to ring and ring. She wished she'd thought to jump in the car, but she hadn't. Her shoes weren't made for walking long distances, especially in dirt and gravel, but she hurried as quickly as she could.

Amber wasn't exactly out of shape, but yoga was a long cry from speed-walking, and she arrived at the homestead out of breath and a bit sweaty. Scarlett stood on the top step, her face shining with joy. Maybe they'd found a birth mother ready to adopt out her baby. Maybe the ranch had hit a milestone.

The excitement hung in the air, and Amber couldn't wait to hear what the news was. The veterinary staff had arrived ahead of her, and Dave leaned closer to Sissy and said something in a low voice. Amber wanted someone to share her life with too, and supreme gratitude descended on her that she was here, at this ranch, with these people.

She felt such love from them, from this family of people who'd come together at this place.

Tears filled her eyes, and she looked around for Lance, hoping he'd come stand by her and hold her hand.

"We're just going to wait another minute," Scarlett called to everyone. "Hudson, ring the bell one more time."

Hudson did as she asked, and then he returned to Gramps's side, a huge smile on his face. Amber couldn't stand not knowing what they were so happy about. Of course, Scarlett had always been so happy for everyone and everything that happened on the ranch, and Amber really looked up to her.

"Ah, here comes our Canine Club crew," Scarlett said, and Amber couldn't turn fast enough to find Lance. Their eyes met, and it was as though every other face faded away.

He came toward her, a smile shining from his eyes.

"Hey," he said, a bit out of breath himself. "Did we miss it?"

She leaned into his body and let him slip his arm around her waist. "Not yet."

Chapter Seven

Lance was keenly aware of Dave's eyes on him. Sissy's too. Heck, even Cook and Gray couldn't stop looking at him and Amber. The whole situation felt surreal, to be honest. But Lance just let Amber take the lead, and she seemed to want to be close to him. He had no problem with it.

"Okay," Scarlett said. "We've rung the bell and waited, because we have double good news. I'll go first, and then Hudson will tell the second part."

Lance had just arrived, but the level of energy in the air filled the sky. He didn't have time to look around and see if Carson and Adele were there, but when he'd heard the bell, he'd expected it to be about their baby.

"First," Scarlett said. "Adele went into labor last night. She and Carson are down at the hospital, where she's just given birth to a beautiful baby boy." Scarlett's face crumpled, and she pressed her lips together.

Slightly in front of him, Amber sighed, and Lance would've had to have been deaf not to hear it.

"They're all doing great," Scarlett said when she'd regained her composure. "Adele doesn't want visitors right now. They should be home in a few days. We'll keep everyone up-to-date via text. She doesn't want to make a big deal out of it."

"But it's a big deal," Sissy said beside him. "Do you think she'll let us ring the bell when we bring Evelyn home?"

"I don't know, sweetheart," Dave said. "We'll ask her, okay?"

Scarlett moved over next to Gramps. "They named the baby James." She put her arm around Gramps. "After Gramps." She looked at the old man with such love. He did wipe his eyes then, and a cheer went up from the crowd. Lance moved away from Amber so he could clap too, the joy and love he felt in this gathering of people so strong it reminded him of family. Scarlett and Hudson had been gracious and kind when he'd lost his father last year, and Lance had never felt this close to co-workers before.

"All right, Hudson," Scarlett said, her voice breaking again. "Your turn."

Hudson took her face in both of his hands and gazed down at her, obviously not caring about the crowd watching. He said something Lance couldn't hear from the back of the crowd, but he could plainly see the love on Hudson's face.

Lance wanted what Scarlett and Hudson had, and he glanced at Amber. He'd been hung up on her for so long, and he sincerely hoped he hadn't been wasting his time.

"All right," Hudson said, his voice louder and carrying easier. "I'll make it short. Scarlett and I have been chosen by a birth mother."

Sissy squealed at the same time several other women in the crowd did.

"We'll be bringing home twins in May."

"Twins," someone said.

"Oh, my goodness," someone added.

"That's amazing," Amber said, turning to him. Her entire countenance glowed. "Isn't that so amazing?"

"It sure is." Lance couldn't even pretend to understand why Scarlett was sobbing, or why Amber said, "I have to go," and started pressing her way through the volunteers toward the front porch.

But he knew Scarlett wanted kids and couldn't have them. He'd seen Jeri and Sawyer adopt, and Dave and Sissy were only weeks away from bringing home their adopted little girl. He wondered if Amber wanted kids, and if she'd be able to have any biologically. He thought of his childhood memories with his father, the teenage memories, the adult memories. He'd loved his dad with every fiber of his being, and a sense of missing hit him so hard, he had to turn away from the scene on the porch.

Lance definitely wanted kids. A boy for sure.

He waited until most of the crowd dispersed. Then he climbed the steps behind Dave and shook Hudson's hand. "Congratulations," he said sincerely. "You two are going to be great parents."

Hudson beamed, still so humble when he said, "I sure hope so." He hooked his thumb over his shoulder toward the front door, where the women were filing inside. "We told Karla early, and she has lunch ready, if you want to come in."

Lance did, his stomach growling and his eyes searching for where Amber had gone. He closed the front door behind him, expecting to see a huge crowd. But everyone from the ranch wasn't there. Just Gramps, Scarlett, and Hudson. Jeri and Sawyer and their son, Brayden. Dave and Sissy. Karla and Cache. Cook, Ames, Gray, and Gina, the lead veterinarian. Lance joined Amber, lightly touching her hand.

She turned into him, pure joy on her face. "Isn't this so exciting? Two babies within a month. And then twins in May."

He grinned down at her. "It's pretty exciting." He leaned closer, hoping he wasn't about to make a big mistake. "Do you want children, Amber?"

She blinked, but the spark and joy in her eyes didn't go out. "I do. You?"

He nodded and faced the group just as Hudson started to speak. "Thanks for coming in. I guess we

64

should've warned you so you could tell your teams and get things lined up for this." He glanced at Cache. "But I guess none of the animals will die, right?" He chuckled. "A big thanks to Karla for making this meal for us to share together. We—Scarlett and I—really feel like you guys are our family, and we love you."

He nodded, emotions storming across his face. "I think Cache has something he wants to say." Hudson moved back, seemingly glad to be out of the spotlight, and Cache stepped forward.

"Karla and I were going to get married in May, but with the twins coming, we've decided to postpone until June. It's going to be right here at the ranch, in that dairy cow field across the street." He grinned out at everyone. "Jeri's going to build us an altar, and we want you all in the wedding party."

Dave whooped, and that set everyone to clapping, laughing, and cheering. Lance once again felt like he'd come home. To these people. To this place.

He thought about his mother down in that house that was too big for her now. The yard she barely worked in anymore. The dog she'd never really liked but couldn't get rid of because Lance's dad had loved him.

An idea started in the back of his mind and grew as people chatted and moved through the line. He slipped away from Amber and over to Scarlett.

"First," he said. "Congratulations." He hugged her quickly. "And second, I have something I want to talk to you about. Maybe I can come later today, when you're not so busy?"

Scarlett continued to smile at him, her eyes turning a bit sharper. "Serious?"

"It's about my mother," he said, the idea still forming and morphing. "I—She's alone at her place, and she'd love it here. The sense of family. The animals. All of it. I'd look after her. She can pay rent."

Scarlett picked up a plate and handed it to him. "I don't see why she'd need to do that when we have thirteen cabins, eight of which are empty. And once Cache marries Karla and moves in with her, there will be nine empty ones."

Lance nodded. The cabins on either side of him were taken, but Cache wouldn't be there past June.

"If she wants to come, we'd love to have her." Scarlett smiled at him. "Is she doing okay?"

"I don't know," Lance said, his mind troubled about her for some reason. "I'll talk to her and my family. See what everyone thinks."

"Just let me know."

Lance said he would, his mind churning now, really digging into the idea. He couldn't wait to call his mom, but he thought he should probably talk to Arthur first. See what his older brother had to say.

He re-joined Amber, and she nodded toward Scarlett. "What was that about?"

Lance told her, grateful he had someone to bounce

ideas off of, and they spent lunch talking about the pros and cons of having his mother live right next door. In the end, he said, "It's Last Chance Ranch. She'd love it here," and he knew he was right.

Everyone who came to Last Chance Ranch loved it. There was something special about the animals here, the way they'd been broken and then rescued. God Himself had touched this place, and Lance felt it more keenly than ever.

Now he just needed to talk to his brother, and then his mom.

LANCE SIGHED as he locked the last enclosure for the day. His back hurt, and his feet pinched, and he was an hour later getting home than usual. Given the excitement over all the babies coming to the ranch, it was fine. But he was tired, and hungry, and in no mood to find Cache, Cook, and Dave sitting on his front steps.

"You guys lost?" he asked as he approached. "I think it's Cache who usually has food in his cabin."

They stood up like they'd practiced doing it together. "Karla did send leftovers," Cache said, holding out a plastic container.

Lance took it with a smile. "Let me guess. You want to know about me and Amber."

"Some details would be nice," Dave said.

"Really?" Lance rolled his eyes, though he was joking. "Like all the details you gave us about Sissy?"

"Hey, I told you we were dating. That's more than Cache did."

"Cache told me, actually," Lance said, glancing at Cache.

"What?" Dave asked. Roared might have been a better way to describe it.

Lance laughed and went up the steps to the door. "Come in. I have bread if anyone wants toast."

"You told Lance about you and Karla?" Dave asked.

"Look, man, it was a complicated thing, and I knew he wouldn't say anything."

"I wouldn't have said anything."

"You kind of lecture, man," Cache said.

"I do not," Dave said.

"So," Lance said. "Why are you here?"

Dave looked back and forth from Cache to Lance to Cook. "I—"

Lance laughed again. "You can lecture me if you want, Dave. I don't care. Cache and Cook helped me with a plan, and I executed it." He looked at the other cowboys, hoping they'd come to back him up not throw him under the bus.

"He executed it *well*," Cache said.

"How many times have you been out with her?"

"Just once," Lance said. "We went to Pages. I see her around the ranch. I have to communicate a lot with her about the adoptions." He busied himself feeding the cats and dogs he'd adopted so he could see Amber more often. Dave surely knew about that, too. The man didn't miss much.

"I didn't come to lecture," Dave said. "I came to say good for you for finally asking her out."

"Hey, I wanted to a long time ago," Lance said. *"You're* the one who told me to wait."

"She had a boyfriend."

"She always has a boyfriend," Lance said, realizing how that made Amber sound.

"Yeah," Cache said, grinning. "And now it's you."

"Maybe," Lance said. "We've been out once."

"She obviously likes you," Dave said.

"Yeah? What's so obvious about it?"

"Besides the way she stepped right into your embrace?" Dave rolled his eyes as he set bread in the toaster.

"So I'm starting the high school track team running thing next week," Lance said. "Who wants to help me?"

No one said a word, and Lance burst into laughter again. "You guys are so helpful."

"Cook wants us to help him with a plan," Cache said. "That's why we came. He saw how well yours worked, and he figured we could help him too."

"Oh yeah?" Lance asked, turning to put his leftovers in the microwave now that his pets were fed. "Who do you want to go out with?"

Cook looked at Cache, who said, "I can't talk for you all the time, man."

"Gina," Cook said, his face turning red. "Gina Weller."

"The vet?" Dave asked. "I thought she was married."

"Divorced," Cook said. "Three years ago."

Lance's eyebrows went up along with Dave's. "So you must talk to her," he said. "To know that."

"He does," Cache said. "But it's fleeting, and she's sort of clueless."

"She's busy," Dave said. "There's a huge difference. And she might not be looking to date, so she's closed off to the opportunity right in front of her."

"So how do we get her to open up?" Cache mused. "That's what Cookie here would like to know." He grinned at the cowboy, but Lance thought Cook looked like he could punch Cache if he called him Cookie again.

"What does she like?" Lance asked. "The doughnuts worked well with Amber...."

"Everything is not about Amber," Cache said. "Let's focus."

Oh, but everything was about Amber. At least for Lance, and he couldn't wait until Valentine's Day when he'd get to take her out again.

Chapter Eight

Amber arrived at the Canine Club to find dozens of people there already. She wasn't late, but she obviously wasn't the first to arrive either.

"Lance," she called when she saw the broad-shouldered cowboy move through the crowd. He turned toward her, caught her eye, and gestured for her to follow him.

"Everyone outside," he said, his voice lifting above the chatter and giggles of the teenagers gathered around. They did what he said, and Amber brought up the rear of the group.

There were approximately twenty runners here, boys and girls. The track teacher wore a jacket with the word COACH on the back in huge, yellow letters, and he moved to stand beside Lance.

He'd kept her up-to-date with everything happening

with this new program on the ranch, but it was exciting to see it all coming together in person.

"All right, guys," the track coach said. "Listen up." He looked at Lance, who gestured to the dogs behind him.

"These are our running dogs," he said. "They love to run and play, and it's your job to make sure they don't get hurt while they're with you. They have to stay leashed at all times." He surveyed the group, his eyes bright with hope, but sober at the same time.

"Coach Tea says you're his best students, and we both expect you to be when you're with the dogs. They have vests on so people can see they're available to adopt. If anyone asks you, just send them up here to the ranch. Our adoption coordinator is Amber Haws." He indicated her, and Amber lifted her hand and waved, glad she had the brainpower to do that. Watching Lance take command like this was incredibly sexy, and she couldn't look away from him.

"We have a route from here down to Balboa Park," Coach Tea said. "It's four miles. For most of us, that's nothing. We'll stay there for thirty minutes with the dogs, and then we'll run back here. You're expected to note your times, like we always do on our runs, but we're not going for personal best today, all right, guys?"

"The dogs will probably influence how fast you can go. We have a couple that like to sniff, but once you get going, they should come along with you." Lance looked behind him again. "I expect you to remember your dog's name and make sure you always know where he or she is."

He and Coach Tea looked at one another, and Amber saw all the hours of work that had gone into this partnership. The behind-the-scenes work it took to put something like this together could be huge, and she appreciated Lance for thinking outside the box and making good things happen for the animals at Last Chance Ranch.

"Amber and I will meet you at the park," Lance said. "We'll have a couple of reporters there, with a photographer. Feel free to talk to them about the experience."

"We do want it to be a positive experience for you and the dogs," Coach Tea said. "So don't say rude stuff, all right, guys?"

The teens nodded, and Coach Tea said, "Okay, then. A few more rules on dog care, and then we warm up."

Lance launched into how to hold a leash. That he'd trained every dog to sit with a voice command and a hand signal. That every runner should have treats in their pockets, as all of these particular dogs were trained with treats and enjoyed them.

"When you get to the park, we'll have balls and Frisbees for the retrieving dogs."

"Ready?" Coach Tea asked.

Lance stepped through the gate while the coach had his team captain come up and start leading the other teens through their warm up. Amber joined Lance, taking the leashes he handed to her without a word.

Her heart bobbed in the back of her throat, and she wanted to tell him what a great job he'd done here. "I talked to Jewel this morning," she said instead. "She said she'd try to be at the park too. If she can't be there, she said she'd send someone."

"That's great," Lance said. "I got Karla to get us a local reporter, so we'll have some media coverage."

"Do you think this will be good for the dogs?"

Lance looked down at the four surrounding him. "Yes," he said quietly. "And the kids. It's going to be awesome." He glanced up at her, those beautiful eyes shining. "Are you worried?"

"A little," she said. "You chose Thunder."

"He's a great dog," Lance said. "He *needs* to run. He'll be fine."

"Who are you going to give him to?"

"The coach," Lance said. "Once he knows what's going on, Thunder will be able to run with anyone."

"It's a brilliant idea," Amber said, dropping her voice. "Getting them visible, socializing, and running. It's the perfect plan."

"The coach called me," Lance said, shrugging. "It's not like I came up with it."

"I know," Amber said. "But you put it all together. I know you did. You just told Coach Tea when to show up and how many people to bring."

Lance didn't argue, which meant Amber was right. She touched his hand. "Are you nervous too?"

He stopped coiling the same leash over and over again. "A little," he said. "I chose Thunder." He looked like he'd swallowed poison for which there was no antidote.

Amber wanted to kiss that anxiety from his face. Instead, she smiled and said, "Coach Tea is a big guy. He can handle Thunder."

Lance swallowed and nodded. "You want to go to dinner tonight?"

"Of course," she said, thrilled he'd finally asked her out again. They saw each other around the ranch every day, but it was nice to take things to the next level romantically off-site.

He grinned and tucked a lock of her hair behind her ear. "I know I said we'd ride together to the park, but I think I'm going to follow the pack in my truck, if that's okay."

"Of course," she said again. "I have all the toys loaded up already. I'll meet you there."

"Okay." He returned to the group and started handing out leashes and dog assignments. The dogs were definitely excited, but no one left until everyone had a dog at their side, properly leashed and under control.

Amber took out her phone and snapped a picture of Lance in front of all of them, his face open and honest and happy.

Then he said, "All right. We'll see you at Balboa Park," and the Coach started off with Thunder. His runners stayed together in a pack, the dogs right there with them.

Amber tapped the video button and managed to get a few seconds of the action before everyone was too far away and dust covered things.

"That was amazing," she said to Lance.

"It really was, wasn't it?" He turned toward her, and Amber didn't stop and think. She didn't wait to analyze the situation.

She stepped into his arms, put her hands on that strong jaw that had been a feature in her dreams, and kissed him.

His hands moved through her hair as he returned the kiss, and Amber's pulse accelerated, zooming through her whole body. Lance took control of the kiss, his mouth soft and insistent at the same time.

Amber sighed into him, and he slowed, his hands moving down her back to her waist as he kissed her sweetly. He pulled away and rested his forehead against hers.

She had no idea what to say. She kept her eyes closed, wishing he'd kiss her again. And again. And again.

Yes, she'd had several boyfriends over the past couple of years. Lance had probably seen them all parading in and out of her life, and a slip of humiliation moved through her.

But none of them had kissed her the way he just had. "Lance—" she said, but he stole the rest of her words with another kiss. She felt passion here. Adoration. Love.

She'd known Lance liked her. The flirting had established that. The doughnuts had testified of it. But this kiss?

This kiss said he cherished her, and for Amber, in that moment, there was no better feeling in the world.

"I CAN'T BELIEVE we adopted out seven dogs today," Amber said as she opened the door to the diner. "Seven dogs, Lance. It's incredible."

"Big dogs, too," he said.

"Seven big dogs." Amber felt like she was inside a movie, one where things just didn't make sense even when they happened.

"Four of those were to track team members." Lance chuckled. "Maybe we shouldn't be so excited." He held up two fingers for the hostess, and she grabbed two menus and led them to a table.

"Hey, I'll take dog adoptions no matter how we get them," she said. "Even Jewel was stunned."

"Maybe we should have them run with cats," Lance said, smiling as he lifted his glass of water to his lips.

Amber burst into laughter. "Can you imagine? Leashed cats, with athletes trying to get them to run." She shook her head, still giggling.

"It would make headlines." Lance shrugged, though he was completely kidding too.

"So, Mister Longcomb. Tell me something else about you I don't know."

He reached for the menu and hid behind it for a moment. "Oh, I don't know. I'm an open book."

"Hardly." She watched him, sure he wouldn't make her work too hard. When he said nothing, she said, "Okay, I'll tell you what I know about you, and you can correct me or add to it. Sound good?"

"I suppose," he said, though he didn't seem terribly impressed with this game.

"You're a cowboy, so you like horses and dogs and animals." She paused when the waitress arrived, and she and Lance put in their orders.

"You love your family, and you go see them every week. You go to church, and you like to play the drums."

"Mm, right there," he said, lifting his eyes from the straw wrapper he'd been tying in knots. "I like to play the guitar. I'm just on drums because no one else could do it."

Amber watched him for a moment. "Guitar, not drums. Got it. You like country music, and well, hamburgers." He'd ordered one here tonight, and one at Pages.

"That's it?" he asked.

"That's what I know." She wasn't going to vocalize how good-looking she thought he was, or how faithful. Those sort of statements would reveal too much of herself, and she wasn't ready to do that yet.

"I like a hot breakfast," he said. "My mother cooked for us kids every morning. Hash browns, bacon, eggs, toast."

"Your dad had a farm, right?"

"A small one," he said. "And here's something I bet you don't know. I like to dance."

Glee lit up Amber like a light bulb. "You do?"

"Yeah, country dancing. Or you know, line dancing."

She laughed, tipping her head back and really laughing. She snorted a couple of times, but she didn't care. Lance joined in with her, and when their food arrived, she said, "I'd really like to see that."

"Let's dance at Cache and Karla's wedding," he said. "Surely they'll have a band there."

"Yeah," she said. "*Your* band."

"No." Lance shook his head. "Cache won't want to play on his wedding day."

"Mm." Amber started mixing the mayo she'd requested with ketchup to make a sauce for her fries. They talked and laughed some more, and everything was so easy about being with Lance.

He took her home and walked her to the front porch again, like he had last time they'd gone to dinner. Tonight, though, he took her into his arms effortlessly and leaned down to kiss her.

"Best day I've had in long, long time," he whispered, matching his mouth to hers once more.

She wanted to say, "Me too," but she just kept kissing him instead.

Chapter Nine

Admittedly, Lance hadn't kissed a woman in a while, but the feel of Amber's mouth against his was unlike anything he'd ever experienced. It was like she'd been made to kiss him, and he couldn't seem to stop himself tonight.

She finally pulled away, breathless and with her hair mussed up around her face. She smoothed it back and smiled at him. "You better get back to the ranch, cowboy."

He nodded, a blip of embarrassment squirreling through him. Everything about this afternoon and evening had just been so perfect. The dogs had behaved beautifully, and the cross-country team had agreed to come get the canines twice a week for their runs.

And Amber had kissed him.

He felt like he'd been lit up from the inside as he walked back to his truck. Before he knew it, he'd arrived back at his cabin. Kicked off his boots. Collapsed into bed right before his phone rang.

"Hey, Art," he said to his brother.

"Lance, I just saw the news with the dogs."

"Yeah?" He sat up, having forgotten about the media coverage already. He fumbled for the remote control, only to knock it to the ground.

"Yeah, it was amazing. You looked good on camera too."

"Thanks." Lance finally got the remote and turned on the TV. They'd already moved on to the weather though. Disappointment cut through him, only intensifying the longer he watched the guy gesture toward clouds and low pressure systems.

"Mom said she recorded it if you missed it."

"I did," Lance said. "I'll watch it when we're out there this Sunday. Are we still going to talk to Mom about coming to Last Chance Ranch?"

"About that...." Arthur cleared his throat. "Sandy and I can't be there this Sunday."

"Oh, okay," Lance said. "Why not?"

"She's not feeling well."

Lance heard something more in his brother's words, but he didn't press the issue. "Okay. Well, do you think I could talk to her alone? Or do you want to be there?"

"Kristen will be there," Art said. "You two talk to her about it."

"Okay." Lance wasn't sure what to say next. "Hey, is

everything okay with you? I mean—" It was Wednesday, and Sandy was so sick she couldn't make Sunday dinner?

"I'm okay." Art sighed, a heavy, heavy sound that made Lance listen harder. "We lost another baby. Sandy is devastated." Art's voice dropped to a whisper. "And she's having some health problems right now, so we're just going to be sticking closer to home this weekend."

Lance's heart skipped a beat, and then two. He loved his sister-in-law, and he loved the two kids Sandy and Art already had. "I'm so sorry," he said.

"It's fine," Art said. "I mean, it's not fine, but we'll be okay. She just needs some time to herself, and time to find the path God wants us on. That's all."

"I understand." If anyone did, it was Lance. He hadn't understood a lot of things about why his first marriage had been such a disaster. Time had helped heal the wounds, as had his family and his faith. But he still didn't know why he'd had to fall so completely in love with Peggy, only to have her make him question everything he'd ever felt for another person.

"What's new with you?" Art asked, another sigh following. "Besides all the dog programs, of course."

"Well," Lance said. "Don't die, but I'm seeing someone."

"What?" Art made choking noises over the phone. "I'm dying. Lance, you can't be serious."

"I am," he said. "Her name's Amber, and things are actually going pretty well."

"That's great," his brother said, sincerity in his voice. A wail came through the line, and he said, "I have to go, Lance. I want to hear more about it. Soon, okay?"

"Yep," Lance said, and the call ended. He didn't need to tell his brother every detail about his relationship with Amber. It was enough to know he had a relationship with Amber.

He fell back onto the bed again, a smile on his face. "Thank you, Lord," he said to the ceiling. "For everything. For the dogs. For Coach Tea. For good food at the diner."

He blinked, thinking of that first kiss with Amber again. "And for Amber. Yeah...thank you for Amber."

LANCE CHECKED one more time to make sure his cats and dogs had food and water. Of course they did. He'd done it an hour ago. Before he'd showered. Before dressing in the black suit he currently wore. Before ordering a bouquet of red roses online to be picked up in fifteen minutes.

He had the reservation at Covington's Steakhouse. He had the ballet tickets in his breast pocket. He literally had everything planned to make this Valentine's Day the most magical one of his life—and hopefully, Amber's too.

Now, he just needed to go get the woman.

His throat felt so dry, and he wasn't even sure why. He'd kissed Amber every day for the past week, and she'd given him no indication that she wanted to stop anytime soon.

His stomach flipped every time he saw her, and when she opened the door to go to the ballet with him was no different. She wore a dark red dress in a color he thought was called burgundy, and it hugged her hips and swelled across her chest. With wide straps over her shoulders, it almost looked like sleeves, and she held her hand out like, *Well?* a sparkly, flirty look in her eyes.

"Stunning," he said, reaching up to adjust his tie. It choked him, but maybe his breathing was getting restricted by the sight of this gorgeous woman in front of him.

She laughed lightly, took the roses from him, and stepped onto the porch, her hands going right to his bow tie too. "You clean up nice, cowboy." She twisted and set the roses on the table beside the front door and then brought it closed behind her.

"Good enough for the ballet?" he whispered.

"You know there will be people there in jeans, right?" she asked, moving back to fiddle with his clothes again. He held very still, because she was so close, and he could barely think.

"You mentioned that," he said. And yet, they'd dressed up as if they were going to a wedding. This was better than what Lance would wear to a wedding. Had worn, especially the few that had taken place out on the ranch.

Sure, he'd dressed up a little. Switched out his work

hat for his church one. Wore his nice boots, all polished up and gleaming. Slacks. White shirt. Tie.

But wearing a suit jacket felt like so much more than that.

She finally finished with his tie and stepped back. "You're very handsome." She stretched up at the same time he leaned down. Their lips brushed, and fire started in Lance's stomach. This felt like their first kiss all over again, and he enjoyed the energy of this date already.

"We'll be late," he whispered against her mouth, but her fingers tightened on his collar and drew him back for another kiss.

He pressed her into her closed front door and kissed her until he couldn't breathe. Heat and desire mixed with embarrassment, but she didn't giggle. Didn't say anything. Just kept trailing her fingers through his hair along the back of his neck.

"Our reservation is in fifteen minutes," he said, finally putting some distance between them. He threaded his fingers through hers and led her to the truck. She waited in the spot next to the steering wheel when he got in, and he reclaimed her hand as soon as possible.

"How's the wedding prep going?" he asked.

"Fine," she said, and Lance wasn't an expert on women, but he knew not to ask about the wedding again.

"I didn't get a chance to talk to my mom on Sunday," he said to quickly change the topic. "Kristen was there, of course, and her daughter fell and busted up her lip."

"Oh, no."

"Yeah." Lance shook his head just thinking of the fuss Tia had thrown. There had been a lot of blood, and Kristen and Joel had ended up leaving early. "I didn't want to talk to my mom alone, so we're going to try for this Sunday."

"Good idea," she said. "Here's a question for you. When do you think I might be able to meet your mother?"

"You want to meet my mother?" Lance didn't mean his tone to sound so shocked.

"Sure," she said. "She's obviously very important to you."

"Yeah." He looked out the window, wondering why this surprised him so much. Maybe because this was technically their third date, though he'd been kissing her for a week now. "Well, she's probably going to move to Last Chance Ranch. I'm sure you'll get to meet her soon."

"Oh, I almost forgot," she said. "I bought you some of that really dark chocolate you like. It's at the house."

"Ninety-three percent?"

"Yes," she said, bringing out the giggle now. It made his pulse ricochet around inside his body, and he liked the pretty sound of her laugh so much. He liked it when she laughed from her stomach too, and the light way she snorted when she did.

Lance liked everything about this woman, and the fact that she'd crawled right into his heart surprised him.

"I don't know how you eat it," she said. "It doesn't even seem to melt."

"It melts," he said. "It's fantastic."

"I'll leave you to it."

"I signed us up for the three-course meal tonight," he said. "It includes dessert, so I'm sure you'll get to have something sweet." He grinned at her, pleased when she smiled back at him.

He pulled into the steakhouse a few minutes later. Walking in with Amber on his arm made Lance feel like a prince, and he couldn't help beaming around at the crowd like *She's with me. Can you believe she's with me?*

No one seemed to question that the gorgeous Amber Haws was with him, and he enjoyed dinner immensely. She ordered a tuxedo cake, with alternating layers of chocolate and vanilla cake, and when she pressed her lips around that fork...Lance felt sure he'd combust.

They laughed and talked, and everything with her was easy, just as he'd hoped it would be. They found their seats in the theater, and she started talking about the ballet in an excited voice.

"When's the last time you went to a ballet?" he asked.

"Years," she said.

"Why didn't you go?" he asked. "I mean, I know you got hurt and had to stop dancing. Seems like you'd still go watch, though. Experience it any way you could."

She considered his words, her eyes glued to the program. "I couldn't feel the joy in the dancing after I got hurt." She looked at him, those wide brown eyes so vulnerable. "At least for a while. After that, I didn't have anyone to go with." She shrugged like that explained everything.

Lance let it drop, though he thought she could've certainly mentioned it to any of her boyfriends over the years. Surely one of them would've taken her.

Soon enough, the lights dimmed, and the curtains opened. Amber's excitement beside him made him smile, and he sent up a prayer of gratitude that he'd been able to be the one to experience this with her. *Please allow her to feel the joy in the dance again*, he prayed.

Ballet wasn't Lance's first choice of things to watch, but even he could appreciate the beauty in the movement. He could tell the dancers worked hard to be at the level they were, and he understood the countless hours behind the curtain no one saw.

Intermission arrived, and Amber stood to clap along with most of the rest of the audience. Lance joined her, his legs not quite short enough to be comfortable in the narrow rows. She turned to him, full of light. "Isn't it great?"

"Yeah," he said sincerely. "I really like it."

"Buy me a soda?"

"Of course." He gestured for her to enter the aisle first, and he followed her up to the lobby, where they joined the line to get refreshments.

Amber pulled out her phone and frowned at it. Lance tried not to look. He did, but his eyes just flew to the screen. Something male in him wanted to make sure Amber never had anything to frown about, and he certainly didn't want anything to ruin their perfect night. Their first Valentine's Day.

He watched as she typed. *He's just a cowboy, Mom. It's nothing.*

The breath left his body as if someone had attached a vacuum to his lungs and turned it on. His eyes caught on the message above the one Amber was about to send.

JJ says you're seeing someone new already. Who is he?

He glanced away as Amber glanced up. His throat felt like she'd poured cement in it, and it was hardening quickly. Unable to swallow or talk, he stood there feeling more and more foolish by the second.

He's just a cowboy.

Amber had dated a lot of cowboys.

It's nothing.

She hadn't kissed him like they were nothing. Just a couple of hours ago, she'd kissed him like they could be married next week and he could do a whole lot more than kiss her.

"Look, they have a cotton candy concoction," she said as if his whole world hadn't just crashed and burned.

He inched forward with her, not wanting to ruin this, but for him, it had already been ruined. Several people waited in the line in front of them, and he had time for a conversation.

"Why did you tell your mom we're nothing?" He

swung his head toward her, catching the surprise and guilt in her eyes. He didn't want to accuse her of anything, and he didn't want her to feel like he'd be spying on her.

He gestured to her phone, still clutched in her hand. "I just happened to see it. I wasn't purposely looking."

Amber blinked and nodded, but she didn't explain. He inched forward, gently putting his hand on her lower back to guide her with him.

"I don't feel like this is nothing," he said quietly. In fact, to him, this was very much something. The biggest something he'd had in his life in almost two decades.

"If you do, that's fine," he said, his courage almost gone. "I just don't think you should kiss me the way you did earlier tonight if what you just told your mother is really true." He removed his hand from her back and put a few inches between them without getting out of line.

Chapter Ten

Amber felt Lance retreating right in front of her. "I'm sorry," she finally said. "I don't know why I said that."

"Sure you do," he said, cutting her a look out of the corner of his eye. "I'm not twenty-five-years-old, Amber. We're adults. If you're not into me, it's fine."

But she was "into him." She was.

Before she could explain that her mother was just too nosy, and Amber didn't feel like sharing tonight of all nights—didn't her mother know it was Valentine's Day? Why was she texting right now?—Lance asked, "How many boyfriends have you had?"

"Ever?" she asked.

"Let's say in the last three years," he clarified.

She hated that he wouldn't look at her. Yes, there were

dozens of people within earshot, and no, she didn't want to cause a scene either.

"A lot," she admitted. Surely he already knew that. He wasn't blind.

"How many?" he asked again, taking another step forward. They were almost to the front of the line, and Amber just wanted to crawl back to her seat and finish the ballet. She wished she hadn't brought her phone at all, though she had gotten a really cute selfie of the two of them at the steakhouse and again sitting in their seats before the show started.

She started counting the men she'd been out with that she would consider a boyfriend. "Nine," she finally said, her voice on the outer edge of a whisper. Had she really been out with that many men?

Yes, she had. She'd been taught it was okay to dip into the dating pool often, really search for the kind of man she wanted. More importantly, by dating a lot, she knew the type of man she *didn't* want.

Lance nodded as if he were a bobble-head doll. "You're the only girlfriend I've had in the past three years."

"Not true," she said. "You went out with Kaylee a few times last summer."

He met her eye then. "Never kissed her," he said. "She was a poor substitute for who I really wanted to ask out." With that, he stepped up to the counter and ordered himself a cola and her the cotton candy concoction she'd spied earlier. She knew it would be too sweet, but right now, she needed the extra sugar.

He paid, waited for the drinks, and handed her the bright blue one with a puff of pink cotton candy on the top of the straw before walking away.

"Lance," she said, hurrying after to him to a spot by the windows. He'd already gulped half of his drink.

"I'm sorry," he said, his voice harder than she'd ever heard it, at least when he was talking to her. "I just—I'm not *just a cowboy*. This is *not* nothing." He looked at her again, his eyes filled with desperation now. "Is it? Am I really that delusional?"

Tears filled her eyes, but she would not let them out. She'd worked too hard on her makeup, and she would not spend another Valentine's Day crying. Not when she had the best cowboy boyfriend right in front of her.

"You're not delusional," she said. Taking a moment to center herself, she drew in a deep breath. "I like you, cowboy. A lot. I like that you're a cowboy, even though I swore them off a few weeks ago." She felt light-headed, but Lance was there. Lance anchored her.

"And this is definitely something," she finished. "I just —my mother is a special person, and I'm struggling with my sister's engagement, and I just didn't want to spend our first Valentine's Day texting her."

Lance's eyebrows went up. "Our *first* Valentine's Day?"

She heard what she'd implied. Lifting her chin, she nodded. "Yeah. Our first, hopefully of many."

Lance blinked a few times. The lights flashed overhead, and Amber hadn't even tasted her drink yet. She wanted a picture of it too. Neither of them moved, and she finally said, "I'm sorry, Lance. Honestly, I don't think this is nothing."

"I know you don't."

She handed him her phone. "Take a picture of me with this drink?" She held it up and put a smile on her face.

He grinned too as he took it, and then she dunked the tuft of cotton candy into the liquid, watching it melt away into nothing. She wished she could do that with the text he'd seen. How could ten seconds change everything so dramatically?

Lance put his hand on the small of her back again, guiding her toward the door. As they joined the throng of people and were forced to slow, he leaned down and breathed in the scent of her hair. His lips touched her earlobe as he said, "Thank you for apologizing, sweetheart."

And just like that, the band of tension that had wound its way around her chest released. Relief took its place, and she pressed her eyes closed in a quick moment of gratitude for a good man who could forgive.

THE NEXT TIME the bell rang, Amber was already at the homestead. She and Karla had been baking all morning, and even Adele had managed to help out by putting a batch or two of cupcakes in the oven.

"They're here," she said, pushing herself off the couch and setting her infant in the bassinet in the dining room.

Amber wanted to run right out to the porch too, but she had a tray of cupcakes to finish icing. She worked faster, Karla chattering excitedly as she detailed every inch of road Dave and Sissy's car touched.

"They're pulling in," she said, and she skipped away from the window to the front door, which stood open from when Scarlett and Adele had gone out there. Amber swirled on the last of the frosting and hurried after her friends, her heart pounding in her chest.

Hudson and Sawyer sat on the front steps while Jeri stood down the porch a bit, baby Brayden perched on her hip. He babbled as if he knew another baby would steal the spotlight from him any moment.

Dave got out of the car, and Sissy bent into the back-seat to get the baby carrier. They both wore a look of love and reverence on their faces, and Amber felt it all the way down in her toes.

"This is Evelyn May," Sissy said, finally turning the carrier so everyone could see. Amber sucked in a breath at the baby's beauty.

"All that hair," Scarlett said with a choked laugh. She

ran down the steps and hugged Sissy. "I'm so happy for you."

Sissy cried openly, the tears a slow track down her face. She looked up at Dave, who just smiled at her and put his arm around her.

"Can we get her out?" Karla asked, and Amber wanted to hold that baby too. She had dark skin and she seemed to be sleeping peacefully. "Or do you not want us to wake her?"

"It's okay," Sissy said, and she set about unbuckling the straps around the tiny human. "I don't really know how to do this...." She giggled, but it was nervous. "Oh, there it goes." She lifted the baby out and brought her right to her shoulder, patting her gently. The baby made a tiny grunting noise, and Amber was in love with her.

More people started arriving, and Sissy ended up keeping baby Evelyn in her arms, showing her around to the volunteers and cowboys and staff who'd come to wish them well. A small pile of gifts accumulated on the lawn, and Amber started writing down who'd brought what so Sissy could send thank you cards later.

She'd get her chance to hold that baby. Maybe not right now, but soon enough. Lance arrived, and he kissed her temple. "Hey, sweetheart."

He smelled like wet dogs, and she looked him up and down. "What happened to you?"

"Oh, one of the bowsers got a little excited today. Had to remind him who the pack leader is." He flashed her a smile, and Amber practically melted under the wattage of it. "Be back in a sec."

He moved over to the happy family and offered his congratulations. Dave held him tight for an extra long time, his mouth moving at Lance's ear.

Lance nodded, and then he bent over and kissed baby Evelyn's forehead before returning to her. "I can't stay. Want to come to my place for dinner tonight?"

"Do you cook?" Her thumbs stilled in the typing of who'd just left the pink baby bag with the rattle on it.

"I'm not half-bad," he said. "You like cheese, right?"

"Who doesn't like cheese?"

He laughed, tipped his hat to her, and walked backward a few steps. "It'll be a little later. Maybe seven-ish? You can come by anytime, though. I'm sure my pets would love to see you." And with that, he was gone again.

Amber watched him go, his long, powerful strides eating up the distance between the homestead and the Canine Club quickly. She couldn't see herself breaking up with him anytime soon, and her heart started flopping like a fish out of water.

She'd never envisioned herself with any of her boyfriends long-term. Lance was definitely different, and she was glad for that.

She was also concerned that she was so afraid of a long-term boyfriend. Of spending her time with the same person for the rest of her life.

Why did that scare her so much?

"Your turn, Amber," Sissy said, appearing in front of Amber. "Did you seriously take notes of the gifts?"

"Yep," Amber said, stuffing her phone in her back pocket so she could take the baby from Sissy. "I'll email it to you." She took the precious bundle and cradled her close to her heart. "Oh, Sissy, she's perfect. Absolutely perfect."

"So you and Lance?"

"Yeah." Amber looked up at her friend. Maybe Sissy could help her understand why she was so scared. "He's great."

"He is." She looked over to the Canine Club, as if she could still see him. "You seem to like him too. Dave says you guys have been dating for a while."

"Five or six weeks,' Amber said.

"That's a long time for you," Sissy said with a grin. "I see how it is." She kissed her baby and added, "I'll be right back, okay?" before walking away.

Amber wanted to call her back and ask her what she saw. She also disliked that five or six weeks was a long time for her to date someone, but the truth was, it was.

She couldn't change that, even if she wanted to.

No, what she needed to change was herself.

Chapter Eleven

Lance pulled up to his mother's house, relieved that Arthur's SUV already sat in the driveway. His brother came out onto the porch before Lance could unplug his phone and get his dogs out of the truck.

"Hey." Lance smiled at him, noticing his older brother had more silver on the sides of his hair than last time. He clapped Arthur on the back and asked how Sandy was doing.

"She's recovering," Arthur said, a flash of pain stealing across his face. "But we got a new puppy. Come see."

"A puppy?" He closed the tailgate on the truck and figured Ribbon and Maddie would be fine in the backyard. They always had been before.

He followed his brother into the house to find his niece and nephew down on the floor with the pup. His mother grinned at them all like they were the greatest things she'd ever seen, and she jumped to her feet when Lance said, "Hey, Mom."

"There you are. I thought you'd come right after church."

"Yeah, I...." He glanced at Arthur, who cocked his head slightly. "I'm dating that woman I told you about. We had lunch together before I came."

Happiness lit up his mother's face, and she said, "Well, isn't that nice?"

Lance ducked his head, because it was nice.

"When do we get to meet her?" his mom asked.

"Mom," Art said, exchanging a glance with Lance. "I'm sure it's still pretty new." He moved over to his kids. "Let's show Uncle Lance the new pup."

Lance smiled at his mom and squeezed her hand before joining the fray in the living room. "What kind of dog is it?" he asked his nephew.

The eight-year-old had teeth that were a little too big for his face, but Devon's smile revealed them all. "A puppy."

Lance chuckled and reached out to touch the black furball. "I can see it's a puppy, bud."

"Her name is Magnolia," Kacey said.

"She's a poodle mix," Sandy said, smiling at Lance. His heart constricted tightly as he looked at her. She seemed happy now, but he knew a well-placed smile and a puppy could cover a lot of emotions.

"We got her from a shelter," Devon said. "I wanted to

come up to your ranch, Uncle Lance, but my dad said it was too far." He climbed into Lance's lap, and a feeling of warmth moved through Lance.

"It's pretty far from your house, bud." He looked at Art. "You got a poodle mix puppy at a shelter?"

"Someone had abandoned all the puppies at a drugstore," he said. "So they had them when we went. She said this one was the last one, and they'd only had them a couple of hours."

He nodded, as that made sense. People liked certain breeds. And puppies? They'd fly out the adoption door.

The puppy barked, and everyone laughed. Lance watched his mother, and she seemed so great today. His resolve to ask her to come live next door to him at Last Chance Ranch slipped, but he reminded himself she didn't always have her grandkids here. She wouldn't always have a new puppy.

It did make a long drive for Art and his family, and Lance knew the move would mean they wouldn't come to dinner every Sunday. Before he could say anything to his brother, the front door opened, and Kristen walked in, her daughter already wailing.

"Oh, what's wrong?" His mother took Tia, and Kristen looked more frazzled than ever. Her husband didn't seem to be fazed at all, and Scott nodded at Lance.

"Come see the puppy, Aunt Kristen," Devon said, jumping up. "Tia, we have a puppy." That got the four-year-old to quiet, and she squirmed out of her grandmother's arms to come see the little dog.

Lance groaned as he got off the floor, his heart suddenly swooping down to his stomach. It was an uncomfortable feeling, and he knew he was about to have an uncomfortable conversation too.

"Mom," he said. "We wanted to talk to you about something." Art came with him as Lance stepped into the kitchen. Only a dozen or so feet separated them from the kids and the dog, but Lance felt so far away in that moment.

"What's going on?" she asked, looking at all three of her children.

Art and Lance exchanged another look, and then Kristen said, "We think you should sell the house. Lance wants you to move up by him at the ranch."

Lance reached over and took his sister's hand, squeezing it gently. Gratitude filled him that he hadn't had to say the words. And now they were out.

His mother looked like they'd each found something to hit her with. She folded her arms across her chest and sighed, her lips trembling slightly. Without saying anything, she moved over to the big glass doors that led onto the deck, and then down into the big backyard.

Lance followed her, slipping his arm around his mom's shoulders. "Rufus would love it up there. There are so many dogs, and we'd take care of him."

"I don't even like that dog," she whispered.

Lance leaned his head against her shoulder. "I know, Mom. There are good people at the ranch. You won't be alone. There's always something going on, and everyone will love you like family."

Art joined them, his eyes out on the farm too. "We won't be able to come as often, Mom, but Lance will be right next door. It's a good move."

"This place needs so much work," she said. "I haven't cleaned out anything."

"So we clean it out," Kristen said from behind them. "I can come help while Tia's at preschool. We can do bigger things on Sundays when we're all here."

Their mother sighed, the sound getting masked when a timer went off. She didn't move to check it, and Kristen went to silence it. "Let me think about it," she finally said. When she looked at Lance, he found fierce determination in her eyes.

"All right, Mom," he said. "Just think about it. I can send you some pictures of where you could live."

"How much?"

He stepped away from her. "It's free, Mom. It's a cowboy cabin in the community where I live. Two bedrooms. It's not nice, but it's not bad. With your skills, you could make it look like a real home." He grinned at her and watched Kristen pull out a sugared ham.

"Time to eat," Art said, calling into the kids and putting an end to the conversation. He turned back to their mom. "I think it's a good idea, Mom. This place is too big for you, and you need a fresh start. You need to be closer to people."

She nodded and ducked into the kitchen to finish getting everything ready for dinner. Lance and Art looked at one another, and Lance shrugged one shoulder.

"I think she'll do it," Art said. "Give her a few days, and then call her."

"I want to hear about Uncle Lance's new girlfriend," his mom said, and he spun in her direction, his heart pounding again but for an entirely different reason.

"Me too," Art said, picking up a plate.

"You have a girlfriend?" Kristen asked. "Why am I always the last to know?"

FEBRUARY BECAME MARCH, and Lance continued his work with the high school cross-country club. He loved seeing those kids on the ranch, as they brought new life and vibrancy to it. They'd adopted out thirteen of the original twenty dogs, and Lance spent a lot of time trying to find other animals they could leash and take to the park.

Some of their dogs simply weren't ready for something of that magnitude. He managed to find five more, and everyone assured him that they didn't all need a dog to run with. They had twelve among them, and that was great.

If he didn't drive to his mother's to help her clean out her house, he managed to spend a little bit of time with

Amber in the evenings. He was glad he had other things to occupy him though, because her texts to her mother about their relationship still burned in the back of his mind.

Not all the time, and with each passing day, they cooled slightly. He'd accepted her apology, and her explanation, but that didn't mean he had to keep showing up to get his heart sliced and diced.

He sure did like her, and she seemed pleased to see him every time he walked into the volunteer house. But he was glad he had more on his to-do list so that he didn't have to constantly ask Amber to spend time with him.

Foolishness hit him from time to time when he realized she hardly ever texted him first. He invited her to dinner, to eat lunch with him, to go on a quick walk with a hyper dog. He went to her house at night, or over to her office in the volunteer house.

She didn't come to him, and as the spring rains came, Lance found himself sitting on the top step of his porch, his guitar in his hands. Strumming mindless chords, he made a conscious decision not to reach out to Amber that day. He had a full day of work on the ranch already, and he was meeting with a real estate agent at his mother's house that evening.

He could text Amber, of course. But he wanted to see if she'd text him first. He almost scoffed at himself. At the test he was giving her, though she didn't know it. How was that fair?

He sighed, ducked his head, and focused on the guitar

strings. He didn't want to feel frustrated in his relationship, but he did.

Memories of his other serious relationships came forward, even as he tried to push against them by singing. He focused on each word as he sang about the Savior, and thankfully, the hard times and bad memories stayed dormant.

Lance had never been one to dwell on the past, and he wasn't going to start now. He finished the song he'd learned long ago at his father's knee, and the resulting silence only reminded him that his dad wasn't there anymore.

"I miss you, Dad," he whispered into the misty sky. The wind picked up as if his dad had heard him and wanted him to know it was okay to feel the way he did.

A car turned into his driveway, and Lance blinked a couple of times before he realized it was Amber. Surprise filled him, and he jumped to his feet. After leaning his guitar against the post, he hurried down the steps into the rain.

"Hey," she said, getting out of her car with a pink pastry box. "I know you have a super busy day today, so I brought fuel."

Joy filled him from top to bottom, and Lance took the doughnuts from her and set them on top of the car. He swept her into his arms, enjoying the squeal of laughter as he lifted her off her feet and spun her around.

"It's so good to see you," he said as he bent down to kiss her.

"It's raining," she said against his lips, but he didn't care. He formed his mouth to hers, a kiss in the rain exactly what he needed this morning.

She didn't protest, and she didn't seem to be hurrying the kiss. In fact, he broke their connection first, and said, "Let's go inside."

He grabbed the box of doughnuts and they both laughed as they dashed through the intensifying rain to the safety of his porch. Snagging his guitar, he led the way into the cabin, where the rush of adrenaline remained after she'd slammed the door behind her.

It wasn't the first time Amber had been to his cabin. But he felt a charge between them that hadn't existed in a while.

He put everything down and returned to where she stood just inside the door, wiping water from her hair. "You came to me," he said, feeling a little out of control. He threaded his fingers through hers as he backed her into the door.

She looked at him with those sultry eyes, a hint of confusion there. "I came to you?"

"I always text you," he said. "I always ask you out."

She tensed, and Lance simply looked at her. "Are you worried—what are you worried about?"

"That...I don't know." He sighed and backed up. "Nothing. It's nothing." He hated the words as they came out of his mouth, because they reminded him so much of her text. If she caught the significance of them, she didn't say.

"Lance," she said, but he turned away and moved into the kitchen.

"Coffee?" he asked.

"No," she said. His floorboards creaked as she joined him. She linked her arm through his and leaned into his bicep. He wanted to be strong for her. Wanted to hold her up and make her feel beautiful.

"I don't want coffee," she said. "I came, because I wondered if maybe you and I could sit together in church this next week."

Chapter Twelve

Amber didn't like the distance between her and Lance, and she needed to remember to write that down. She'd been talking to someone through a counseling app, and the therapist had suggested she take note of how she felt about Lance, no matter what it was.

Through her muddled thoughts, she'd realized how much she enjoyed her time with him—and how much more she wanted in a relationship with him.

She'd never done that before, and while she felt strong and brave most of the time, it had taken her almost a week to work up the courage to show up at his house with pastries and a question about church.

That he still hadn't answered.

"It's fine," she said. "I know—"

"Of course I'd like to sit together at church." He pressed his lips to her forehead. "And I think it would be great if you wanted to meet my family before my mother moves here."

Fear struck Amber right in the back of her brain. "Sure," she said anyway, and she wondered where the word had come from. She'd already asked to meet his mom, but he'd acted like it was too soon. A few weeks had gone by now, though, and the fact was, his mom would be moving into the cabin in the corner by the beginning of April.

Hopefully.

"Do we want to do all of that in one day?" she asked. "Church in the morning, and then dinner out at your mom's? Everyone will be there, right?"

Lance nodded, turning to take her fully into his arms. "Yeah, everyone will be there."

Amber pressed her cheek to his chest, listening to the strong beat of his heart. "Lance, I've...I've been kind of an idiot in the past."

"What do you mean?"

"I mean, I dated nine men in three years. And that didn't even count the ones I went out once or twice." She stepped away from him, her nerves assaulting her now. "I—I don't know what I was looking for. I'm afraid I still might not. I—I don't know." She felt so mixed up. So torn in half. So put together wrong.

"I'm talking to someone," she said. "I'm trying to make sure I don't lose—" She clamped her lips around the words. Lance had probably heard them anyway. She didn't want to lose him. Didn't want to lose a good man, perhaps the way she had in the past.

But she didn't want him to think she wanted to get back together with any of the men she'd dated in the last three years. She didn't. She just didn't want to throw him away if he was the one.

In fact, until Amber had started talking to Kevin through the app, she hadn't even believed there *was* a one for her.

"Who are you talking to?" he asked gently.

"It's through an app on your phone or computer," she said. "I can chat or text, and he'll call me if I want him to. His name's Kevin Forrest. He's licensed and stuff."

Lance's mouth made a tight line, but he didn't say anything.

"I think it's been helping," Amber said. "And maybe, if you'd like, you'd want to come meet my family too."

Lance lifted his eyes back to hers, his expression glinting and yet still so serious. "Really?"

"Of course." She smiled at him, wishing he'd relax a little bit. "That's what people do when they date."

"That's what people do when they're seriously dating," he clarified. "Are we seriously dating?"

Amber felt like he'd swung a punch at her. "I mean, I thought we were. *Are.* I think we are. Don't you?"

"I do," he said. "I just wasn't sure you did."

"Well, I do." Amber took a deep breath, her mind spinning her thoughts away from her. "Lance, I've spent most of my life trying to please my mother. Nothing I did, no grade I ever got, no boyfriend I've ever had, was good enough for her." She sighed, not really sure where she was going with this.

"She's a great lady," she said. "But...I don't know. I just —I think I've made a bigger deal out of some things in my life, just to get her attention. Prove that I'm valuable somehow."

"What kinds of things?"

"Oh, you know. Bad break-ups, or getting jobs I wasn't really qualified for." She emitted a shaky laugh. "Did you know before I came to Forever Friends, I was running a sports club?"

He blinked, a slow smile finally spreading his mouth. "You don't even like sports."

"No, I don't." The tension between them finally felt like it had cracked. "Not only that, I don't know anything about sports. Or running a restaurant. Or hiring people. Or anything. It was a huge mess."

She put both hands on his chest and moved them up to touch his collar. "I'm much better suited for the job here, and it was actually a relief when Forever Friends assigned me here. But I've been doing a pretty good job of messing up my personal life for a long time." She tipped up on her toes and pressed her mouth to his for a quick kiss. "Can you be patient with me while I sort it all out?"

"Sure," he said huskily. "I waited two years to ask you out. I feel like I can wait for anything."

She giggled, glad when he finally truly put both arms around her and held her close to him—right where she always wanted to be.

THE WEEK PASSED QUICKLY, and before Amber knew it, Sunday had arrived. She dressed carefully, making sure her skirt wasn't too tight and her blouse was clean and pressed. She chose appropriate earrings for a woman her age, and didn't put on too much make-up. She didn't have anyone to impress at church, but afterward, Lance would be driving her to his childhood home to meet his mother, brother, and sister. His two nieces and one nephew, and all his in-laws.

Nervous was an understatement, and Amber took off the bright pink blouse she'd chosen and started rummaging through the closet for a different one.

In moments like these, she needed a girlfriend. Someone who could come over and calm her down. She had a couple of women she sat by at church normally, and she quickly pulled out her phone to text Edith.

Meeting Lance's mother today. Which blouse goes with my navy pencil skirt the best?

She stood in front of her clothes, feeling very removed from reality. She hadn't met a man's family in a long, long time. Her relationships didn't normally progress that far.

Her mouth felt so dry, and she jumped when her phone chimed.

That pink one, Edith had said. *How exciting!*

"The pink one," Amber muttered as she pulled it back off the hanger. She put it back on and buttoned it up with trembling fingers. She needed to learn how to trust her own feelings, her own instincts.

She didn't understand why she couldn't do so in her personal life. She had no problem making decisions and trusting her gut at work.

She'd just finished slipping her feet into her heels when Lance knocked on the front door. "Coming," she called, hurrying to grab her phone and shove it in her purse. A moment later, she pulled open the door to find her handsome cowboy boyfriend standing there.

He wasn't as dressed up as he'd been for the ballet, but her breath still hitched somewhere in the back of her throat. Lance grinned at her and extended his hand toward her. She eagerly slipped hers into his, and said, "I've had a new idea for goat yoga. Will you tell me if it's stupid?"

"I'm sure it won't be stupid." He helped her up into the truck through his door, and then climbed in beside her.

"Full moon yoga," she said. "With the goats, of course."

"So yoga at night?"

"Yeah," she said. "And only once a month. So it would

116

be a special class. Yoga under the light of the full moon. Maybe for couples-only."

"Do men actually come to goat yoga?" he asked as he set the truck toward the little church they attended at the base of the bluff.

"Tons," she said. "You should try it, cowboy. You've been so tense lately."

"I have not," he said. "I just work too much."

Amber reached over and took his hand in hers. "I know." She squeezed his fingers, beyond happy when he squeezed back. This moment between them felt so simple and yet so real. "I'll talk to Adele about the full moon yoga."

"I think it sounds like a good idea," he said. "Couples only. Like, date night at the ranch."

"Right," she said. "Cache is doing that cow cuddling now, and Karla totally has that geared toward couples." Amber needed to talk to her about the idea too, but for now, she just enjoyed the scent of Lance's shirt, the strength in his hand, the sound of him singing along with the song on the radio.

Amber sighed, realizing how very much she liked this man. She'd been going to this church since she'd relocated to Last Chance Ranch, so walking in felt normal. Of course, walking in with her hand in Lance's was new, but no one seemed to notice.

They'd arrived a few minutes early, and Amber checked her phone while the choir sang up on the dais.

She frowned at a message from Jewel. *Need to meet this week. What's your schedule like?*

She tipped the phone toward Lance. "She has to text me on Sunday?"

"What does she want to meet about?" he asked.

"I have no idea," she said, tapping quickly to tell Jewel to pick a time, and Amber would accommodate the schedule.

Tomorrow morning. First thing.

Great, Amber sent back, feeling nervous all over again. She pressed her eyes closed and sent a prayer up. *Please let this be a good meeting. I've been doing all the paperwork right. What could it be this time?*

She'd never heard a voice or felt like God had yanked her in a specific direction before. But today, sitting in the pews and waiting for church to begin, Amber felt a very keen sense that God loved her. No, she didn't know what the meeting was about. But it didn't matter.

God loved her.

Her feelings about relationships were all messed up and tangled. But she'd figure it out, because God loved her.

Tears sprang to her eyes, and she let the anxiety and restlessness and impatience with herself fade away under the warm blanket of that love.

Thank you, she thought, mouthing the words. Lance lifted his arm and put it around her shoulders, and she opened her eyes and leaned into him.

"Okay?" he asked.

"Okay," she said, because she was.

A couple of hours later, she could've used another dose of peace in her life. She sat in Lance's truck outside his mother's house, a small, two-story structure that sat in the middle of a huge piece of land. Lance had called it a small farm, but Amber thought he'd underestimated.

"Here we are," he said. "That's the tree I planted in third grade." He pointed to the huge maple in the front yard and got out of the truck. "It's going to be hard to move my mother out of this place."

Amber slid out of the truck, immediately taking his hand. Mostly for herself, but she sensed he could use some grounding too. "Why don't you just take over the farm?"

He flinched and met her eye. "I...can't." He moved to the back of the truck and let his dogs out, unfolding the steps for Ribbon so the dog didn't have to jump.

"Why not?" she asked. "You know everything about ranches and farms. You're the best cowboy ever." Why was he at Last Chance Ranch when he had access to all this land? "Your mother could stay here with you."

"I'm not the best cowboy ever." He shook his head as he smiled. "And I don't want the farm out here. It's not worth anything."

"More than living in a cabin on land you don't own."

Lance tensed, and Amber had just decided to drop the subject when he nodded toward the front door. "There

119

she is." He secured his hand in Amber's again and lifted his free hand in a wave. "Hey, Mom."

She came down the steps, and she radiated warmth in the depths of her blue eyes. Lance's were a shade or two brighter than hers, and her hair had probably been blonde in the past. Right now, it held a lovely shade of silver, and Amber smiled at her.

"Mom, this is my girlfriend, Amber. Amber, my mother, Jamie Lee."

"Hello, dear." His mom received Amber right into her arms. "You're just beautiful, aren't you?"

Amber grinned as she stepped back. "Thank you."

"That's what I tell her," Lance said, smiling too.

"I don't know how you got her to go out with you." His mother laughed, stepping to his side and linking her arm through his. "Of course, you're quite the catch too."

"Strange how no one's snapped him up yet," Amber said, and a flicker of fear flashed across Lance's face. Oh, there was a story there, and Amber hadn't heard it yet.

"Well, someone did," his mom said. "Years ago. But it has been a while since Lance has met anyone special."

"Years ago?" she asked as they reached the top of the steps.

"Mom," Lance said. "I haven't told her about Peggy yet."

His mother's eyes opened wide, as did her mouth. "Oh, I'm sorry. I just assumed—I'll go put on the coffee."

"Mom—" he started, but she bustled away, the front door closing quickly after her.

"Peggy?" Amber asked playfully. "You've never mentioned anything about your dating history." And she'd never asked. She supposed she'd just assumed—as his mother had—that Lance had been the way he was now. But she wasn't, and she hardly recognized herself when she looked in the mirror now, after only a couple of months of dating Lance. So why she thought he'd always been the man he was now didn't make sense.

"I was married to Peggy," he said, the words like bombs in Amber's ears.

Chapter Thirteen

"Married?" Amber sounded like she'd inhaled helium.

Lance sighed, wishing he'd prepped his mother better. It wasn't her fault in the slightest. "For nine months," he said.

"Oh, my goodness." Amber covered her mouth, her eyes wide. "Did she have a baby?"

"No," he said quickly, shaking his head. "No. I don't have any kids." He paced back to the top of the steps, annoyance flowing through him. "She was simply someone very different than I thought she was. We got divorced, and I haven't dated a whole lot in the fifteen years since."

Amber joined him, but she didn't touch him the way he wanted her to.

"That's all," he said. "That's the whole dating history.

I mean, I went out with a few women here and there. No one I'd say I was dating." He stared out at the tree his father had helped him plant.

Amber's questions about the farm here were warranted. They were very good questions. His mother hadn't even suggested he try to buy and take over the farm when he and his siblings had talked to her about moving to Last Chance Ranch.

He sighed, this day feeling heavier than he'd like it to. "And I can't move out here and run my father's farm. My mother doesn't own it. When my father was sick, she and my dad sold all the land to the guy next door to pay for the treatments. He let them keep the house and stay living in it."

The sign the real estate agent had put up swayed in the breeze. "So she's just selling the house, and honestly, we offered it to Alan Swenson, who bought the land, and he'd putting together an offer."

He faced her. "No one wants a house without land." Lance included. "I'm fine at Last Chance Ranch. I love it there."

"I do too," she said. "I'm sorry. I didn't know."

"It's fine," he said. "It's my fault for not telling you. Some things are just hard to talk about, I guess."

"You're not especially loquacious," she teased.

"Ha ha," he said, feeling like he talked a lot. Said exactly what was on his mind. "Come on. Let's go put my mother out of her misery."

Inside, his mother bustled around the house, setting mugs beside the plates and silverware she already had on the counter. She looked up, her eyes full of nervous energy, when Lance and Amber came in.

Lance deliberately laced his fingers through Amber's so his mother would know everything was fine. "When are the others arriving?" he asked. "And wow, Mom, this place is spotless."

She smiled. "It helps when half of what you own is in storage." She motioned for them to join her in the kitchen. "Come have coffee. Kristen and Art won't be here for another hour or so."

Amber exchanged a glance with Lance before she moved ahead of him and into the kitchen. "Tell me about your husband," she said. "Lance has said great things, but I feel like I barely know him."

Lance tensed, because his mother didn't talk about his dad all that much. But today, she practically glowed as she said, "My Jonathan was wonderful. His biggest flaw was his undying love for dogs. Big dogs."

Amber blinked at her for a moment, and then she burst out laughing. "Lance must've gotten that gene. He loves big dogs too."

"Big dogs have a big spirit," he said, almost defensively. "And Amber trains goats for goat yoga, Mother, so don't let her lead you to believe she's not an animal lover."

"I do," she said. "And I am. But there is something to be said for a small lap-dog, isn't there?" She leaned into his mom as the coffee was poured, and Lance marveled at her easy-going nature, the charisma floating off of her.

He felt more attracted to her than ever, and his heart-beat skipped around inside his chest. Extra stimulant wouldn't help, so he waved off the coffee and went for the banana bread his mother had laid out instead.

The conversation was easy as his mother continued to tell Amber about Lance's father, the farm he'd worked, and pretty much his whole childhood. He only had to say, "Mom, come on," twice, and each time had made Amber giggle like a schoolgirl.

He did like that sound, and by the time his brother arrived with his family, Lance felt like his nerves had been on a hot griddle for hours. He jumped to his feet and headed toward the door as his niece and nephew entered with their puppy.

Art and Sandy both looked past him to where Amber sat with his mother, despite Lance's efforts to speak to them. "She's pretty," Sandy whispered, still gawking at Amber.

"Come meet her," Lance said. "Hey, guys." He scooped Kacey into his arms, causing her to emit a shriek and a giggle. "This is my girlfriend, Amber."

She stood up and tucked one of her curls behind her ear.

"My favorite niece, Kacey. And my favorite nephew, Devon."

"He'll say Tia's his favorite too," Kacey said with a

grin. She also wrapped both hands around Lance's neck, and that wasn't all that comfortable.

"*Two* nieces?" Amber said. "Well, Uncle Lance sure is lucky, isn't he?"

"Do you have nieces?" Kacey asked, her big eyes going wider.

"I sure don't," Amber said, taking the little girl from Lance. "You're going to have to teach me how to be an aunt."

She looked from Amber to Lance. "She has no nieces."

"Shocking," Lance said with a smile. He beamed at Amber too, and she put the little girl down.

"Go steal that puppy from your grandma," she said. "I want to play with him."

Devon ran ahead of Kacey, both of them arguing over who would bring Magnolia to Amber, but Lance's mother already had the dog, and she simply handed the squirming pile of black fur to Amber.

She giggled as Magnolia licked her face, and she quickly handed her to Devon so she could face Lance's brother and sister-in-law.

Lance saw her wipe her hands down the front of her skirt, a sure sign of her nerves. He stepped to her side and took her hand, squeezing it to let her know he was there, and everything would be fine.

"My older brother, Art," he said. "And his wife, Sandy."

"So nice to meet you," Amber said, her smile perfectly

placed. She shook both of their hands, and everyone seemed to be made of grins that day.

"Kristen's late, as usual," Art said.

"She's not always late," Lance said. "But Tia—my other niece—has been having a lot of meltdowns lately."

Sure enough, when Kristen came through the door, Tia was already crying. "My mother will rescue her," Lance whispered, and he and Amber watched while his mom dashed to the door to get Tia and Kristen straightened her shirt.

She made a beeline for Amber, taking her into a hug. "You must be Amber."

"And you're Kristen."

"My husband, Scott."

He and Amber shook hands, and awkwardness descended on the group of adults.

"Lance says you're a dancer," Kristen said.

"Was," Lance said quickly.

"Guilty," Amber said with a light laugh. "But I broke my foot when I was twenty-five. It ended that career."

"Can you have a career as a dancer?" Art asked.

"Oh, sure," Amber said. "I was in the San Francisco Ballet Company. We get paid, just like anyone else." She tucked her hair again, and Lance had never noticed her doing that while she was nervous, but maybe she had.

No matter what, the meeting had gone well, and he said, "Mom, are we ready to eat?" Because the sooner they ate, the sooner they could leave, and Lance could find out what she thought of his family.

Hours later, he finally said, "We should get back to the ranch," with a knowing look in Amber's direction. She had solidly beaten everyone at card games, and Devon was now on a mission to find a game she wasn't good at.

She stood and hugged his mom, who said something quietly that Lance couldn't hear. He shrugged into his jacket while Kristen told him how amazing Amber was, adding, "You better not let her get away from you. She's so much better than Peggy."

"Anyone would be better than Peggy," Lance muttered, flipping the collar of his jacket out so it lay right.

"She's right," Art said, handing Lance his keys. "She's great, Lance. We're happy for you." He smiled at Lance, and Lance drew his brother into a quick hug.

"I'm glad you guys like her." He glanced over to Amber, who was crouched down in front of Tia, saying good-bye. "I *really* like her."

"Oh, I can tell," Kristen said.

"That obvious, huh?"

"Well, just judging on how many women you've brought home to meet us, I'd say yes. But seeing you with her? You two were made for each other." Kristen sighed, always bit on the dramatic side.

Amber stood and walked toward them, and all the good-byes began. Lance finally got her out the door, closing it behind him. A long, hissing sigh came from his mouth. "Wow."

Amber simply laced her arm through his, and they walked back to his truck. "So," he said once they were buckled and on the road. "What did you think?"

Chapter Fourteen

What did she think?

Amber didn't know where to start. "They were fantastic," she said slowly, trying to organize her thoughts. "Everything a family should be, Lance. You're very lucky to have them."

He glanced at her. "What do you mean?"

"I mean, not everyone has a family like that." Amber didn't want to talk negatively about her own family. They were hers, and she didn't know any different. Until now.

Now, she knew families could be warm and loving. They could talk about real things and care about each other. They could laugh and lose and win and share experiences without getting hurt feelings or running off to their bedrooms.

"Lance, my family...isn't like that. I can't remember

the last time I was at my parents' house where someone didn't yell at someone else."

"What? Really?"

"Really," she said quietly, her mind filling with the unpleasant memories. "I wish I could've met your dad."

He tensed beside her, his fingers clenching and unclenching on the steering wheel. "My dad was great," he said, his voice thick with emotion. "He would've loved you, just like everyone else in my family does. And you would've loved him."

"I'm sure that's true."

"He loved animals, especially horses and dogs. When he found out I was at Last Chance Ranch, he told me he wished he could come see it." Lance chuckled. "My dad was so sick when I got hired on there, but I sent him dozens of pictures. He'd have adopted every dog I showed him, if not for my mom."

Amber loved listening to him talk about his dad. What would she say about hers? He stayed out of things. When her mother started in on her or JJ, her dad disappeared down the hall. When JJ accused Amber of something, he'd make coffee and keep his mouth shut. When Amber disagreed with anyone about anything, he'd suggest a movie they'd all seen before.

He was good man, too. Faithful. Employed at the same company for thirty years before he retired.

"We're going to add Rufus to the Club when my mom

moves to the ranch," Lance said. "What paperwork do we need to do that?"

Amber pulled herself out of her mind, as it wasn't a great place to be at the moment. "I'll look into it," she said, snuggling into his arm and drawing his hand off the steering wheel so she could hold it. "Thank you for taking me to meet your family."

He pressed his lips to the top of her head, and said, "Of course."

THE NEXT MORNING, Amber arrived at the volunteer house thirty minutes earlier than usual. Jewel had said *first thing* for their meeting, and she didn't want the leader of Forever Friends to know she sometimes waltzed onto the ranch closer to nine than eight.

She put her lunch in the mini-fridge in the room in the back of the house and got her laptop open and ready. She searched the Forever Friends internal database for the incoming animal form and started filling it out for Rufus.

Jewel walked into the house, her phone stuck to her ear, precisely at eight o'clock. Amber rose from her desk, the form forgotten as she listened to the end of Jewel's conversation. She didn't sound happy, and she told whoever she was talking with to "make it right," before she hung up and looked at Amber.

"Hello, dear." Jewel was an older woman, and she had

a grandmotherly feel to her that was completely different than Lance's mother. Less friendly, for one. And Jewel had eyes that could judge in a snap, while Jamie Lee was kind to the core.

Of course, Jamie Lee wasn't running the largest animal rescue non-profit organization in the country either.

"What's going on?" Amber asked as she pulled her chair around the desk to the side. Jewel sat in the chair on the other side, a sigh radiating from her whole body.

"An opportunity has come up," she said.

Amber simply focused on listening, because her heart was beating so loudly, she could barely hear her boss.

"It's a huge job, and a big promotion, but I think you'll be stellar at it." Jewel grinned, those all-knowing eyes softening with the movement of her mouth.

"A new job?" Amber asked. "For me?"

"Yes," Jewel said. "You have on your employment forms that you're willing to transfer, and we have a brand-new facility opening outside of Denver. It's four times as big as Last Chance Ranch, and you'll be the Adoption Director, over a whole team of people who do what you're doing here." She sounded absolutely delighted.

All Amber could hear was *transfer*.

Outside of Denver.

She felt like she was falling. A silent scream started in the back of her throat and ripped through her body, making breathing difficult.

Jewel started talking again, but Amber couldn't discern words. The other woman bent over and pulled something out of her bag, handing the folder stuffed with papers to Amber. She blinked, trying to find her center, as she flipped open the folder and started reading.

The salary was twice what she was making here. She got a housing allowance. Money to relocate. And a team of nine adoption consultants, one for each area of the ranch with animals to adopt out.

Her mind spun with the possibilities, with how many animals she could help on a rescue facility of that size.

But in the back of her mind, a voice had started to cry, and it could only say one thing: *What about Lance?*

His mother was moving to Last Chance Ranch in a matter of weeks. He loved it here, and he wouldn't want to go to Denver.

Would he?

She'd been dating him for a few months. How could she ask him to do that if they weren't married or engaged?

So get married or engaged. The thought dashed through her mind. There one moment and gone the next. It was a ridiculous thought, but Amber couldn't identify why. She was on fragile, new ground with him every day. She couldn't drop this bomb on their relationship.

"What are you thinking, dear?"

Amber looked up from her lap, her thoughts scattering. "I...don't know."

"It would be a big change," Jewel said. "The facility

won't be finished until fall, at the earliest. I'd like you to fly out there when needed, though, to consult on a few things."

Consult.

Amber didn't know if she should nod or what. She could only stare. "I need some time to think about it. Can I have some time to think about it?"

"Of course," Jewel said, though she was clearly surprised.

"My job would still exist here at Last Chance Ranch, wouldn't it?" Amber asked.

"Yes," Jewel said, settling back into her chair and narrowing her eyes at Amber. "Why would you stay here over taking this promotion?"

"This is a great ranch," Amber said.

"It is," Jewel agreed. "But this is a huge step up in the organization, Amber. You've been with us long enough to get these opportunities before someone else."

"I know." She nodded. "I just—my family is here, and I've loved working here, and I just need some time to think about it."

"All right," Jewel said, a hint of dubiousness in her tone. "Let me know."

"When would I have to move to Colorado?"

"Honestly? I've seen the construction plans, and they're ambitious. My guess is not until next year. January, most likely, even if they're not quite finished."

January.

"Thank you, Jewel." Amber came to her senses, and time seemed to be flowing normally again. She shook Jewel's hand, and the woman left the volunteer house. Amber stood in the middle of the room, wondering what in the world to do.

She prayed for that exact knowledge, but no answer that she could understand came. One look at the paperwork on her desk told her she wouldn't be working there that day. She was too keyed up, and she switched out her sandals for a pair of running shoes she kept in the back room for when she had to walk around the ranch.

Barely remembering to grab her cellphone, she headed outside, away from the walls keeping her thoughts and feelings captive. The sun shone overhead, a clear testament that summer would arrive in California sooner rather than later.

Amber loved springtime on the ranch, and she walked slowly, letting her feet take her wherever they wanted to go. She passed the pasture with sheep in them, little babies sticking close to their mothers. The horses had been put out today too, and they shared a pasture with llamas and potbellied pigs.

She loved this ranch. How could she leave it? She had friends here—real friends—that she loved and cared about.

Something told her if she didn't take this promotion, she probably wouldn't get another opportunity for a while. If ever.

She looked at her phone as if buzzed, more out of habit

than a direct instruction from her brain. Lance had asked, *How was the meeting this morning?*

Of course he would ask. He paid attention to her, and knew her, and cared about her. Amber didn't know how to answer, so she just slipped her phone into her skirt pocket. She remembered the overwhelming feeling of love from church yesterday, but she couldn't grasp it today. With every step she took, she wondered what she should do.

Eventually, she found herself entering the gate to the Canine Club, seeking out Lance. He'd help her work through every option and make the best decision possible.

She had to ask a few volunteers where she might find him, and she finally heard he was working in enclosure eight, the one furthest from the gate. The dogs that weren't ready to be with other animals or meet people lived back here, through another gate that had to be locked at all times.

Amber stood at the gate and waited, because she didn't have a key to get through. She didn't want one, as some vicious barking filled the air. A few moments later, Lance's beautiful bass voice lifted into the air, and Amber felt those pieces of her heart flying toward him.

He finally came out of the enclosure building and saw her. "Hey," he said, surprise in his voice. "What are you doing here?"

"I need to talk to you," she said, her insides quaking with nervous energy.

"All right." He pulled on the door handle to make sure

the enclosure was locked, and then he came down the dirt path to the gate. He fitted in the key and started to unlock it.

Amber's impatience grabbed her by the throat, threatening to squeeze the words from her mouth. "Jewel offered me a promotion," she said, her voice just a tiny bit froggy. "It's in Denver."

Lance froze, his eyes meeting hers.

He was so handsome, and so much the cowboy she'd dreamt about having in her life. And suddenly, the chain-link fence between them felt like miles of impenetrable distance.

Chapter Fifteen

"Denver?" Lance repeated, so many alarms sounding in his mind he could barely think.

"Denver," she said. "Not until January, probably."

He finished unlocking the gate and stepped through it, sensing she needed someone to hold her and tell her everything would be okay. He gathered her into his arms, and she fit there so perfectly. She clung to him, her shoulders shaking as she started to cry.

"Shh," he said, though he was still working through some of the initial shock. "It's okay. Don't cry, sweetheart. It's fine."

"It's not fine," she said into his chest. "You're not going to leave Last Chance Ranch."

He couldn't argue with that, and he had no idea what to say. She quieted quickly and stepped back, wiping underneath her eyes. "Sorry," she said, sniffling. "I'm fine. I just—don't know what to do."

"Did they give you a choice?" he asked.

She nodded. "Yeah."

"So you don't have to go."

"It's a huge opportunity for me," she said.

He nodded, because she was right. "Of course it is."

"What would you do if you were me?"

Oh, he wasn't going there. The thought of Amber not working on this ranch sent daggers right through Lance's muscles. All of them. "I don't know," he said.

"Lance." She clutched one of his hands with both of hers.

Out here in the wilds of the Canine Club, Lance felt isolated. He felt like he could say things he might not say anywhere else, because no one would overhear them. Then he could pretend he'd never said them, and everything would go on as normal.

"Amber," he said calmly though his pulse was rioting. "I've only been in love one other time, but I think I remember what it feels like." He smiled at her, hoping she wouldn't freak out and run away. Run to Denver.

"And I'm in love with you, or pretty dang close. I don't want you to go to Denver."

Love shone in her eyes too, and Amber wound her hands around to the back of his neck and kissed him. "I don't want to go to Denver either."

"Then don't go," he whispered, claiming her mouth

again. He wanted her to stay right there in his arms. Move into his cabin with him. She didn't have to work if she didn't want to.

Amber sighed as she pulled away and tucked herself right into Lance's chest. "Okay, I'm not going to accept the promotion."

"Okay," he said, though a twinge of unrest pinged through him. He didn't want to be the one to steal an amazing opportunity from her, and he prayed that all would work out for her—for them—so they could stay together on this ranch.

LANCE SEEMED to work non-stop as spring continued to bloom around the ranch. He'd accelerated the training with the dogs, trying to get several more road-ready for the cross-country team. Their adoptions had really picked up since that program had started, and Lance simply needed more dogs available for adoption.

Not only that, but Cache was insisting the Last Chance Cowboys play at his wedding. Apparently Karla wanted the band, and Karla was getting everything Karla wanted for the wedding.

Because of that, the band practices had intensified. Lance didn't mind, because it got him out of his own and away from the dogs, both good things in his opinion.

He didn't like being idle. Too much time on his hands,

and he'd start to think of how he'd practically told Amber he loved her. He couldn't believe he'd said that, but even more shocking was that she hadn't run away.

She hadn't said it back either.

It's fine, he told himself as he walked down the street from his cabin to the one in the corner. His mother would be moving in soon, and while Hudson had originally lived in this cabin, no one had inhabited it for a while.

Lance had cleared everything out of it, because his mother was bringing her own furniture. It would be a miracle if it all fit, so the normal furnishings had to be moved out. Scarlett had told him to just put them in a cabin that wasn't being used, and he'd loaded them all into the one next door, where Carson used to live.

Tonight, he was going to fix the back door and make sure all the lightbulbs worked. Amber had been stopping by on her way off the ranch in the evenings, and if he worked in this cabin, she just kept him company.

She hadn't said anything else about the promotion, and he wondered if she'd told Jewel yet that she wouldn't be taking it.

Maddie barked and settled into a growl, but Lance hardly glanced at her. "You live on a ranch," he told her. Sometimes the little dog got all worked up about nothing, and sometimes her high-pitched yips startled him.

Ribbon lifted his head and gave Lance a look like, *Are you going to check on that? No? Okay, I'll go back to sleep.* He laid his head back down, a soft snuffle coming from his throat. Lance smiled at the dogs and went back to reaching as high as he could to remove the lightbulb from the can light in the ceiling.

A moment later, the cabin door opened, and Maddie started barking like a felon had entered.

"It's just me, you silly thing." Amber crouched down and let the little dog jump at her, her tail wagging. She giggled and patted Maddie while Ribbon heaved himself to his feet and went to greet Amber too.

At least he was silent about it.

"Hey," Lance said over his shoulder.

"How are things going in here?" she asked.

"Great." He finally got the bulb out. "Did those curtains come in?"

"Yeah," she said, moving toward him. "I'm going to get them hung before your mother moves in."

"Thanks." He took her easily into his arms, tucking her close to him and surveying the cabin. "Just a few more days."

"I'll bring up groceries on Friday too," she said. "Then she won't have to worry about that over the weekend."

"Mm." Lance pressed his lips to her temple and tried to imagine his mother living here. "I hope this is a good thing."

"You're still worried about it?"

"A little," he admitted. "What if she hates it here?"

"I don't see how that's possible," Amber said. "And

Karla cooks a lot, so she won't even have to do much. There's no yard care. Hardly anything."

"Exactly," he said. "What is she going to do all day?"

"She can volunteer," Amber said. "We always need people in places around the ranch."

"She likes cats," he mused.

"There you go." Amber wrapped her arms around his waist and sighed.

"Did you talk to Jewel?" he asked.

Her grip tightened and then she stepped away from him. "I haven't, no."

Lance frowned, trying to figure her out. "Why not?"

"I don't know."

Lance hated that answer. He'd noticed that Amber said it a lot, though. Maybe she really didn't know. "Well, you don't want the job, right?" It had been almost two weeks since her meeting with Jewel. Why wouldn't she just tell her boss she didn't want the job?

Doubt gathered in the back of his throat, making swallowing difficult. He moved away from her, putting his back to her so she wouldn't be able to see the emotions on his face. He didn't want to see hers either.

"No, I don't want the job. I'm just...."

"Afraid to let it go?" Lance flipped a switch, and all the lights in the kitchen came on except for the one he'd removed. He started unwrapping a new lightbulb.

"I guess," Amber said. "This is going to sound so stupid to you."

Lance simply worked on screwing in the lightbulb with his fingertips, listening.

"In the past few years, I haven't dated anyone as long as I've been dating you."

His fingers slipped, and he grunted as he tried to steady the lightbulb. "Really? It's been three months."

"You know it's true." She sighed and walked back toward the dogs, who'd flopped near the front door. She peered out the window overlooking the porch. "So I'm just...I don't know what. My friends said maybe I shouldn't pass up the job, because we might break up."

Lance gave up trying to get the lightbulb in. "What? You want to break up?"

"I don't, no," she said, her voice barely meeting his ears from all the way across the cabin.

"But just in case," he said, a measure of bitterness coating his voice. He left the kitchen and joined her at the window. "Amber."

She didn't look at him, and frustration lit him up. "Amber," he said again, this time putting his hand on the side of her face and gently leading her to look at him. "Do you think we can't make it?"

Her big brown eyes didn't waver. Didn't fill with tears. "I don't know, Lance. I've never...had a relationship like this, and I just don't know."

"Well, what does your heart say?"

"That I think too much."

Lance smiled, glad when Amber's lips curved up

147

softly too. "You do think too much, sweetheart." He looked out the window too. "January is a long way off. I suppose no one knows what will happen by then."

He knew what he wanted to have happen. But he also knew better than most that what he wanted and what reality was didn't always match up. If they did, he'd have asked Amber out and had this relationship two years ago.

At the same time, he felt like Amber was keeping all of her options open—including the door she'd walk through to leave Last Chance Ranch. And him.

Just in case, he thought.

In case of what? he asked himself. In case she gets bored with you, came to mind. Or she finds someone else who excites her more.

Lance knew he wasn't terribly exciting. He also wasn't going to leave town and call her on his way to break up. He had no idea what she wanted from him, and he suspected she didn't even know what she wanted.

"I'm sorry," she said.

"For what?" he asked.

"For not knowing."

"Can't know the future," he said, but he did know how he felt, and he wanted Amber in his life for good. Permanently. Always.

But she was obviously nowhere near ready to hear that, and he'd practically said it already. *You will not say it again*, he told himself.

"Want to take me to dinner when you're done here?" she asked.

"Sure," he said brightly, hoping he could paste on a happy face while he spent time with the woman he loved. "I shouldn't be too long."

Amber kissed him, and Lance felt the emotion behind the action. She liked him. Problem was, she just didn't know how much or how long it would last.

Chapter Sixteen

E dith handed Amber a plate with the words, "I can't believe you're still with him. He must be The One."

Amber rolled her eyes. She hadn't spent a ton of time with her friends in town since the New Year—since breaking up with Dwayne and starting a relationship with Lance. She worked a lot, and spent most of her free time with Lance, but with his mother moving in the following morning, he'd gone to stay with her for the night so he could load as much as possible into the truck tonight.

His family would be coming to help tomorrow, and Amber was already nervous about seeing them again.

"I like him," she said.

"And yet you didn't tell Jewel no to the new job."

"She hasn't even asked again," Amber said. "It's fine.

You and Katrina made it sound like I'd be stupid to reject the job so soon."

"I'm just saying," Edith said as she scooped a piece of pizza onto her plate. "You don't normally date men this long."

"Lance isn't like other men." As soon as Amber said the words, they rang with truth. Right through her whole soul. Like the experience she'd had in church a few weeks ago, she just knew the truth of them.

She knew God loved her, and she knew Lance wasn't like other men.

Tell Jewel you don't want the job.

The thought moved through her mind slowly as she bit into her supreme pizza. The woman she was now held onto things "just in case."

The woman she wanted to be made decisions and stuck to them. She didn't live in fear of the future, or of her mother being upset with her, or her sister achieving something she hadn't yet.

"Oh, I didn't tell you about Chaz."

"You sure didn't," Amber said, letting herself get distracted by her friend's first date disaster. She laughed and shook her head in all the right places. She asked Edith what she was going to do about him.

"I mean, I can't have every meal at the grocery store," Edith said, lifting her eyebrows. "Right? I mean, he didn't even want to take me to a restaurant. We literally ate lunch from the sample tables."

"He doesn't sound like The One for you."

"Yeah, he's not." She shrugged, because her dating adventures were as varied as Amber's. "He was fun to talk to on the app, though. I can't believe you never tried it."

"Never had to, I guess."

"Yeah, you've got hot cowboys knocking on your door every other day." Edith gave her a knowing look, and Amber just giggled.

"There are a lot of men up at the ranch," she said. "Come volunteer. Several single cowboys still."

"I think I'm going to take a dating break, actually," Edith said, surprising Amber. In the two years Amber had lived on the cute street with the tall trees, Edith had been the only one to date as much as Amber.

They'd become fast friends, and they debriefed with one another after all first dates, no matter what time it was.

"A dating break?"

"Yeah, like you were supposed to in January." Edith cocked those eyebrows again, but Amber couldn't apologize.

"He brought me doughnuts," she said as if that explained everything.

"And you've liked him forever."

"Not forever," Amber said. She and Lance did have some flirting history, and she suddenly thought that she'd liked him for a lot longer than three months. More like nine months, and that catapulted him above anyone she'd ever dated.

THE NEXT MORNING, before she got in her car and drove up to the ranch to help Lance's mother move in, she texted Jewel.

I'm going to have to pass on the job in Denver. It just isn't the right time for me. I hope you understand, and thank you for thinking of me.

She read and re-read the words, just to make sure they were all spelled right and that they sounded professional.

With a deep breath holding in her lungs, she sent the message. As she let her breath out slowly, a sense of absolute contentment moved through her. This was the person she wanted to be. One who went after the man she wanted instead of waiting for him to come to her with a box of doughnuts and a gallon of milk.

Her phone buzzed, but it wasn't Jewel. Lance had said, *Art's driving the truck with my mother, and I left early to get to the ranch ahead of them.*

Everything go okay last night and this morning? she asked.

Great, he said.

See you soon. Amber almost added a heart emoji, but she wasn't sure if she was quite that woman yet. Then she grabbed her keys and headed out, feeling lighter than she had since Jewel had shown up in her office a few weeks ago.

"Moving day," Amber said when Lance opened the

door to his cabin. "The cabin is spotless." She stepped into his embrace and held on tight. Her heart felt like it was tearing into tiny pieces, and she was giving him another shred with every day that passed.

"I hung the curtains, and I made sure there are groceries for tonight." She stepped back to find a hint of anxiety in Lance's blue eyes.

"Thanks, sweetheart," he said, his attention already somewhere else.

"Hey, is everything okay?" she asked, looking over her shoulder too.

"Fine," he said. "Everything is set for Rufus?"

"Yes," she said. "Your mom just needs to sign the form, and I left it on the counter in her new place. He can go right over to the Canine Club when he gets here."

Lance nodded, finally focusing on her. "You want coffee?"

"I thought you'd never ask." She smiled at him, reaching up to touch his face before he could move further into the house. Time stilled as they looked at one another. "Lance, I told Jewel I wasn't going to accept the new job."

A smile filled his whole face. "Really?"

Amber closed her eyes and nodded. "So kiss me before your family shows up, and we have to get to work."

He did exactly what she said, and Amber enjoyed the slow, round way he kissed her before taking her hand and leading her into his kitchen, where he not only had coffee, but a couple of boxes of doughnuts too.

Several minutes later, a horn sounded, and Lance practically jumped out of his skin. "They're here."

Amber followed him out of the house and down the steps. They walked up the road together, hand-in-hand, and she hugged his mother, who looked like she'd been crying.

"Morning, Mom," Lance said as a couple of other cowboys showed up to help her move in. "This is Dave and Sawyer. They're both in the band. Cache too." He nodded to the blond cowboy who came jogging across the lawn.

"Hello, boys. Oh, I feel like I know all of you." She hugged them all. "You have the new baby girl, right?" she asked Dave, and Amber marveled at how she could remember that. It seemed like there was a lot going on around the ranch these days, and Amber felt like she could barely remember things.

"Yes, ma'am," Dave said.

"Thanks for coming to help."

"Wouldn't miss it."

"Mom," Lance said, drawing on her elbow. "This is Ames. And Cook. Gray had to be out in the pasture today. Hudson and Scarlett are coming. And there's Carson with Gramps."

"Gramps?" Amber shaded her eyes as she looked down the road. Sure enough, Hudson and Scarlett strode toward them easily, but Carson stayed back with the older gentleman. "He can't really help, can he?" she asked Hudson as he arrived

"He wouldn't stay home," Hudson said. "He can sit in the shade." He smiled at Lance's mother and shook her hand. She hugged Scarlett, tears pouring down her face now.

"Thank you so much for letting me come live here," Jamie Lee said.

"It's fine," Scarlett said. "It's empty, Jamie Lee. You might as well be living in it." She beamed at her, and then Lance.

"My brother," Lance said. "Arthur. His family is coming to help too."

"They had to stop for gas," he said. "And Kristen texted to say Tia is having a meltdown, so they'll be a little late too."

"Well, we have plenty of help," Amber said, looking at Lance. "So let's get your mom moved in."

He smiled at her, all traces of his nervous energy gone. Art opened the back of the trailer, and Amber linked her arm through Jamie Lee's. "Come on, let's go inside. You can tell them where to put everything as they bring it in."

She led Jamie Lee up the steps and into the cabin. She paused, glancing around. "This is nice," she said. "Lance sent me pictures, but it's hard to see until you're here."

"We put up curtains," Amber said. "To make it feel more homey. And he's checked all the lightbulbs, all the doors.

Everything is ready for you." She stepped over to the fridge. "I got a few groceries for you. Everything is ready." She pressed her lips together, realizing she'd repeated herself.

Why she was nervous, she wasn't sure. She just wanted Lance to be happy—and his mother. Change was hard, Amber knew.

"Thank you, dear." Jamie Lee turned as Lance came inside with a couple of boxes.

"Tell us where, Mom," he said, holding up the line of men ready and willing to work.

"I labeled them," Jamie Lee said, and Amber stepped forward to help too. "Those go here in the kitchen."

Lance moved, and Amber told Cache, "Those go in the spare bedroom. The one on the right side of the hall."

Box by box, and piece by piece, everything got unloaded off the truck and moved into the house. Amber, Kristen, Sandy, and Scarlett started unpacking boxes and putting things away. With the truck empty, the cowboys tipped their hats and got back to their regular jobs around the ranch—all except for Lance.

He stayed in the living room with his mother and the rest of his family. "Mom, I'm going to take Rufus now," he said quietly.

Amber straightened from a box she was unpacking in the kitchen.

Jamie Lee nodded, kneeling down to take the huge dog into a hug. Amber went over to her and helped her stand, keeping her hand in hers.

"I'll go with you," she said to Lance.

Jamie Lee sniffled, and Lance clipped a leash to Rufus's collar. "Be back in a few minutes, Mom. Kristen."

"We're fine here," she said. "Take your time."

Amber followed Lance and Rufus out the front door and down the steps. She wanted to comfort Lance, who had tension radiating from his shoulders. But she knew sometimes a situation just required silence and time to overcome, so she slipped her hand into Lance's as she kept Rufus's admission papers to Last Chance Ranch gripped in the other.

Chapter Seventeen

L ance's mother seemed to settle into her cabin well enough. She didn't come out for a few days, and then he got a text from Amber that said, *I just assigned your mom a room in Feline Frenzy today!*

A smile lit him up, and he knew things would only continue to improve. A week passed, and they went to church together. Karla made her first big meal of the spring, and Lance found his mother behind the table, helping her to serve everyone, when he showed up.

And near the end of April, when his mother had been on the ranch for almost a month, he got a text from Carson that said, *Gramps and your mom are sitting together on his back porch.*

Lance stared at the screen, trying to work out how he felt about that. "They're probably just friends," he said to himself. After all, Gramps was at least a decade older than Lance's mother. Maybe more.

That's great, he sent back to Carson, because he didn't know what else to say. She hadn't talked to anyone in the house, so for her to be here, among all these people, was good. She needed friends, and everyone here worked— except for Gramps. It was a good friendship, and Lance wasn't going to worry about it being more than that. There'd be no point anyway.

May arrived, and with it, all the pollen and allergy- inducing spores. Lance stocked up on medication and sometimes he wore a bandana around his nose and mouth as he worked. The sun started to heat the days for longer, and before he knew it, the entire ranch was holding its breath.

Because Scarlett and Hudson had left for the city a couple of days ago, and they were bringing home their twin boys that afternoon.

Adele, Amber, and Karla had been cooking since Scar- lett had left, and everyone on the ranch was invited to the homestead for a huge party. It wasn't what Lance would want to do if he'd been gone for a few days and now how two babies to take care of. But Scarlett had always made a big deal out of happenings on the ranch, and she'd been waiting to be a mother for a long time.

So Lance found himself smashed into a corner of the homestead with dozens of other people at the appointed time.

"They're coming," Adele said, lifting her phone. "Jeri said they just passed Prime."

The excitement grew, and a few people spilled out onto the front porch, as if seeing Hudson's truck first was important. Amber came over to Lance and sat beside him, her face aglow.

He took her hand and brought it to his lips. Things between them had been going great, especially once she'd truly chosen him over the job in Denver. He hadn't even realized he needed her to make that choice, but he had.

He wasn't sure what had prompted her to do it, but he didn't care. He'd noticed she was different than usual, and he wondered if the online counseling was helping. She hadn't made big changes, but she seemed more confident around the ranch, and he hadn't heard her say anything negative about her engaged sister or her mother in weeks.

She'd been out shopping with them, and JJ had asked Amber to go with her to choose the flowers. Neither experience had upset her, though Lance had expected them to. He hadn't asked her, because he didn't want to imply she wasn't a great person before.

She was.

He'd liked that woman, but he *really* liked this one. He hadn't admitted it to himself yet, but deep down, he knew he was in love with her.

"Two babies at once," he said. "What do you think of that?"

"I think I could barely handle one," she said with a smile.

"I'm sure you'll be a great mom," he said.

"You think so?"

"Sure," he said. "Why wouldn't you be? At the very least, you'd always know where the diapers were."

She laughed and leaned into him, and Lance lifted his arm and put it around her shoulders. "This might not be a great time to talk about this, but have you thought about getting married? I mean, do you want to get married? I mean—" He forced himself to stop talking.

Amber straightened and looked at him. "Are you asking me to marry you?"

"No," he said quickly. "I mean—I'm just asking if you want to get married in general."

"That's usually how it works," she teased. "You get married and *then* have the babies."

"I know," he said. "I just...you've never said."

She gazed at him, so much being said without words. "Yes," she said. "I want to get married."

"It's just...you never dated anyone for very long." Lance didn't know why he was still talking, especially when Amber's eyes sharpened.

"I was taught that I could date around," she said. "Really get to know what kind of man I liked. So...I guess maybe I took that a step too far." She smiled, but it was strained along the edges.

Before Lance could apologize or say anything, the

front door opened, and Hudson entered the homestead, one baby in his arms. Behind him, Scarlett carried the other blue bundle. Amber jumped to her feet and hurried toward them as a cheer went up.

Lance joined in the clapping and congratulating, because it was an amazing thing to leave one day without children and come home with two. Amber was a few years younger than Scarlett, and he wondered if she'd be able to have kids of her own.

He watched her hug their friends and take the baby from Hudson. Adele stood on a chair and announced that the food was ready, and everyone should come eat it while it was hot. Lance vacated his chair and migrated toward Amber, who gazed down at that baby with pure love shining in her face.

"He's beautiful, isn't he?" Amber looked up at Lance with such hope in her eyes.

"He sure is," Lance said. "What did they name them?"

"This one is Miles," Amber said. "The other one is Logan."

Scarlett hadn't given up Logan yet, and Lance didn't blame her. His mother joined them, stroked her finger across baby Miles's forehead, and looked at Lance. "When are you going to have grandbabies?"

"Mom," he said, heat rushing to his face. "I'm not even married."

"You two better get working on that," she said with a

smile, no hint of shame or apology anywhere, and turned to get in line for lunch.

Lance looked at Amber, mortified. But she simply started laughing. After pressing a kiss to the baby's cheek, she said, "I guess everyone is thinking about marriage today." She followed his mom, leaving Lance to wonder what she meant.

Was she thinking about marriage? Getting married to him, specifically?

And if so, why did that make Lance's heart prance in such a strange way?

LIFE around the ranch marched forward, and June announced its arrival with a thunderstorm and strong winds that had most of the cowboys fixing something that had been blown over or had something blown into it during the night.

The Canine Club was no exception, as it had miles of fences keeping dogs where they should be. And wind and fences didn't normally play well together.

Lance made sure he went and got Rufus each morning, and he took the dog with him as he did all his chores around the Club. Rufus had started running with the cross-country team, and he didn't bark nearly as much as he had out on the farm.

Days passed, and fences got fixed, and Lance spent

time with his mother and his girlfriend. Things felt stable and steady, and it all made Lance uneasy for some reason. He almost felt like the ranch was in the space of time where everything was quiet and perfect just before a huge storm.

He didn't want to be negative, and he didn't worry about things until they happened, but he woke each day with a certain tension in his muscles that testified of hard things to come.

Not that June was here, all the excitement of a wedding arrived too. Cache and Karla were just a few weeks away from tying the knot, and the pasture that usually housed his cows started getting spruced up for the big event.

The animals were moved to a new field, and the skeleton of the tent structure started to take shape over the area.

His mother had a doctor's appointment that day, and he tried to focus on the dogs he was working with and not what she might be learning. She'd had some health problems in the past, but nothing too serious. She'd get some medicine, and she'd have a few rough days, and things would get better.

Lance suspected that some of her health concerns came from her mental state, especially after the death of his father. Some of her bad days were simply emotional and mental, and Lance tried to be there for her in the evenings when he could.

He didn't hear from her by lunchtime, and he walked home with the summer sun overhead, wishing for the colder days of December. Of course, when it was December, then he'd wish for the warmer days of June.

"Lance."

He looked up at his name to find his mother sitting on his steps. She'd been crying. "Mom." He hurried toward her and wrapped her in a hug. "What's wrong? What did the doctor say?"

She'd been experiencing a lot of stomach problems, and she hadn't been able to keep much down for about a week now.

"He says it's probably a problem with my gallbladder," she said into Lance's shoulder.

"Oh, well, gallbladders aren't vital," he said.

"It's surgery," she said. "And I have to stop taking my blood thinners, and there's a risk for that, and I'm just nervous."

"I know." Lance kept his arm around her as they walked up the steps. "Have you had lunch?"

"I can't eat anything with fat in it," she said.

"No fat?" Lance didn't even look at the labels on his food. "What about like...?" He couldn't even fill in the blank as his mind emptied. "I think I have a protein shake."

"I'm fine, Lance." She sat on the couch, and she certainly wasn't fine.

"I'll look up what you can eat." He turned toward his

kitchen table, where he kept a laptop he used from time to time.

"The doctor gave me a sheet," she said. "It's mostly vegetables. White rice. Stuff like that."

"I'll come this weekend and help you get things stocked up."

"Lance, you don't need to do that. Kristen and Sandy are coming."

"Did you invite Amber?" Lance knew she liked doing things with his mother, and his mom had her number.

"I did, but she can't come," his mom said.

"I wonder why not."

"She said she was going out of town."

Lance froze, unsure of what he was even doing. "What? She is?"

"Yeah, she said she was going to Denver."

The word seemed to echo in his ears. *Denver. Denver. Denver.*

His mom sighed and she leaned her head against the back of Lance's couch. He needed to call Amber, but he wanted to do it in private.

He should eat first, as he was hungry, but he said, "I'll be back in a minute, Mom," and he strode down the hall, his phone already out as he navigated to Amber's text string and practically punched the call button.

Chapter Eighteen

A mber heard her phone ringing, but she'd left it near
the entrance to the cat enclosure where she'd been
called. One of their rescue cats had tested positive for the
cat flu, and she'd put a ton of volunteers in Feline Frenzy
today to get the cats who'd been infected quarantined
from those that weren't.

Everything had to be cleaned, and enclosures had to
be identified for the sick cats, and Amber's exhaustion hit
a new high before lunch. She didn't have time to eat, or
take phone calls, so she handed another healthy cat to
Kelsie and said, "Enclosure two."

The air conditioning worked, but it wasn't up very
high, and Amber ran the back of her gloved hand over her
forehead as Tricia brought in another cat to be tested.

Gina, the large animal veterinarian, took the cat from
her and gave her to Mariah, the small animal vet. Amber

provided an extra set of hands, as most cats didn't take to being held down or poked and prodded.

"She's the last one in this enclosure," Tricia said as the cat hissed.

"Thanks," Amber said, holding Sabrina the cat on her front side while Mariah got her blood. Several minutes later, the test came back negative, and Amber handed her to Kelsie with "Enclosure two," again.

"Lance is here," Kelsie said, nodding out into the reception area of the cat enclosure. Every one had a full kitchen, as some of the cats had special diets, and Amber couldn't see out into the other room.

He was probably the one who'd called too. She sighed, though she was glad he'd stopped by. He'd probably heard about the cat flu and wanted to see how she was doing.

She followed Kelsie and the yowling Sabrina out into the main room and said, "Hey," to Lance while she went to wash her hands in the kitchen area.

He didn't respond, and he looked like one of the cats they'd been testing all morning. Caged. Angry. Ready to hiss.

Amber stalled. "What's wrong?"

"Can we talk privately?" he asked, his bright blue eyes shooting fire.

"Sure," she said more brightly than she felt. "Let me wash up first."

He nodded and then ducked back outside, leaving Amber to wonder what the big deal was. She hurried to wash her hands, and she joined him out in the heat. "What's going on? How was your mother's appointment this morning?" Maybe that had him upset.

"She needs to have her gallbladder out," he said. "Listen, she said you were going to Denver this weekend." He looked at her with accusation in his eyes.

"Yeah," she said. "I told you about it last night."

He frowned. "No...I don't think so."

She stepped back to the door and grabbed her phone from the shelf inside. "Yes, I texted you while we were talking. I said Jewel asked me to go, because they haven't found anyone else for the job yet, and they need someone who understands the organization." She tapped and swiped, getting to their string of texts she and Lance had exchanged.

"Here it is." She turned her phone toward him so he could see the *looong* purple box where she'd typed it all out. "I thought it was kind of strange you didn't even answer me."

"I did not get that text." He pulled his phone out too, some of his anger leaking off of him. He tapped and swiped too, turning his screen toward her. The message wasn't there.

Amber didn't know what to make of it. "I sent it."

"I can see that." He exhaled and turned away from her. "My mother told me, and I may have freaked out a little bit."

"Why would you freak out?" Amber stepped around

him, feeling very much in control—which was new for her. Usually the man was in control as she freaked out during hard conversations.

She liked this change in herself too. "I'm not staying. I didn't accept the job."

"How long will you be gone?"

"A week. I'll be back in plenty of time for the wedding. I would never miss Karla's wedding."

Lance ducked his head, his fingers darting over to brush hers. "So maybe I freaked out about nothing."

"Why don't you tell me what you freaked out about, and I'll let you know?"

"I thought maybe you'd decided to take the job. Leave me here. Move to Denver and start a new job."

Amber blinked, not liking his words one little bit. "Why would I do that?"

"I don't know." He sighed. "I feel like...maybe this life isn't exciting enough for you. Isn't that one of the reasons you moved through boyfriends so fast?"

Amber fell back a step, stunned now. "I don't know what you're talking about."

"I'm worried I'm not going to be exciting enough for you." Lance stuck his hands in his pockets, pressing his lips together like he'd said too much. He put his head down, and Amber couldn't see his face.

"Lance." Frustration moved through her. "What makes you think I need an exciting life?"

"I don't know," he said. Mumbled, really.

"Amber, Mariah needs you." Kelsie left as fast as she'd opened the door.

"I have to go," she said. "I'm flying out in the morning. Come have coffee with me before I go." She put her hand on the doorknob.

"What time?" He lifted his head to meet her eyes.

"Early, cowboy. As early as you can stand, I'll already be up." She smiled at him and ducked back into the cat enclosure to the sound of at least three cats harmonizing as they howled. "What's going on?" she asked.

Kelsie pointed to the door. "Feline leukemia virus."

"Are you kidding me?" Amber's heart pinged around in her chest. "That is not what we need right now." She didn't see how she was going to leave Last Chance Ranch in less than twenty-four hours. Not in the state it was currently in. But Jewel had promised her she'd send out a new volunteer coordinator for the week, and she'd insisted that she didn't have anyone else to send to Denver.

Amber hurried over to the door and stuck her head inside the makeshift exam room they'd been using. "What do you need from me?"

"We need to close Feline Frenzy," Mariah said. "Immediately. No more tours through here, and we need to contact anyone who's adopted a cat in the past two weeks."

Amber felt the weight of her workload increase, but she nodded. "Are you two okay here for now?"

"Yes," Mariah said over another cat wail.

"I'll go pull the records and start making phone calls."

Amber woke the next morning, actually surprised she'd gotten any sleep at all. She'd been at the ranch until well past dark, and that was saying something for it being summer. She hadn't packed yet, and not only that, the clothes she needed weren't even clean. So she'd been up forever, waiting for the machines in her life to get the stains out of her blouses and skirts.

By the time she'd fallen into bed, all she could think about was Lance, and if he really thought he wasn't good enough for her. She wondered what she'd done to make him feel that way, and her mind had gone round and round and round....

Groaning, she got out of bed and into the shower. Dressed and ready, she padded down the hall to the kitchen to put the coffee on. No sooner had she flipped the switch did someone knock on her front door.

Hurrying, she crossed through the house to pull open the door. Lance stood there, looking devilishly handsome at such an hour. "Hello, cowboy."

"Hello, yourself." He smiled at her, all of the suppressed anger and frustration from yesterday gone. "Early enough?" He let his gaze drip down her. "You're already ready to go."

"I have to leave for the airport in forty-five minutes,"

she said, stepping back to let him in. "So you're right on time."

"I brought doughnuts," he said. "Let me grab them from the truck." He jogged back out to his vehicle, and brought in a small box that only held six doughnuts. A sense of warmth filled Amber, and she held him tight for a moment before busying herself by getting out mugs, and sugar, and cream.

They sat down at the counter together, the silence between them comfortable. "Listen," he said. "I just wanted to apologize about yesterday. I—don't know what."

"Freaked out," she said, lifting her maple bar to her lips. She tried to smile around the mouthful of dough and frosting, but it was impossible.

He chuckled. "Yeah, maybe a little. It's just bad news usually comes in threes, and when I heard you were leaving town, that sort of felt like the third thing."

"What were the other two?" she asked. "Your mom, obviously."

"Yes," he said. "And I got a call yesterday morning that someone wanted to adopt Rufus."

"Oh."

"They have a big ranch, and he'd be happy there."

"Lance, if you don't want to let him go, don't let him go," she said. "You could adopt him or just keep him in the Club."

"He loves to run with the cross-country kids."

"He can still do that."

"Yeah, I know."

Amber sipped her coffee. "So when you heard I was going to Denver, you thought that was bad news number three."

"Yeah," he admitted. "I did. I thought you'd grown tired of me and wanted to break up." He hid behind his own coffee mug, finally lowering it so she could see his eyes.

"Why would you think I was tired of you?"

He shrugged, a ruddiness entering his cheeks. "I guess I feel like we've...stalled."

"Stalled?" Amber's eyebrows went up. "What do you mean?"

"I mean, we took so many steps in the beginning, and now it just feels like, I don't know. We're dating, and then what?"

"You want to get engaged." She wasn't asking, and she watched as several emotions ran across his expression. Fear, hope, embarrassment.

"I don't know," he said.

"Well, I'm not going to ask you," she said. "I'm more traditional in that regard." She couldn't even imagine being engaged. She'd never taken that step. Ever. Her heart started beating frantically, as if he were down on one knee right now.

"Would you say yes if I asked you?"

Her alarm went off, signaling it was time to get loaded up and get to the airport. She picked up her coffee mug as she stood, drained the last swallow of coffee, and plucked another doughnut from the box. "I'm taking one of these with me."

"Amber," he said, following her over to the dishwasher. "Would you?"

"Guess you'll have to ask to find out." She grinned at him, tipped up on her toes to kiss him, and then added, "Now go on, cowboy. I can't miss my flight."

THE FACILITY in Denver was going to be amazing. Downright fantastic. With every sketch and concept she saw, Amber found herself wanting to be there for all of it. She'd spent the first five years of her post-ballet career on the corporate side of secretarial work, where her business organization degree worked well in departments like human resources and accounting. She'd moved from company to company every year or so, learning different things and different policies.

She'd moved over to Forever Friends eleven years ago, stemming from the love she had for animals—and a Strut Your Mutt event she'd attended in Portland while she was there visiting an old college roommate.

She didn't remember what she and Cleo had done. But she remembered those volunteers. Those dogs and cats on leashes. The general positivity she felt at the event, despite the drizzling rain.

It took her another six months to get hired on, and she'd been working with them ever since. She'd been all over California at various positions and placements, but never out of the state. She didn't remember checking that little box on her employment forms that said she was willing to relocate.

"So we'd have an office building—house—for each area," Orion said. He was the lead construction manager, as well as the consultant for Forever Friends on the physical properties side of the company. "What do we need to staff that, Amber?"

"Well." She examined the blueprints, another of her loves coming to life. She could look at building plans for hours and never get bored. "If each house is going to run their own adoptions, you at least need a volunteer coordinator like me. The bigger animals don't have nearly the volume of volunteers or people willing to adopt a lame horse or a pig with a health condition. You could probably assign one person over a couple of animals in those areas."

"What do you wish your volunteer house had?"

"Outdoor signups," she said quickly. "Though here in Colorado, you'll be dealing with snow sometimes. But it would be nice for those people who've been to the facility before to be able to simply sign in, pick the job they've done before, and go. There's too much paperwork for repeat volunteers."

"That sounds like an organizational issue," Roman said. "I'll note it for Jewel though. We're anticipating twice the volume of volunteers here than you have at Last Chance Ranch."

Amber nodded and flipped the page on the plans. "What's this area here?" She pointed to a separate building that looked very much like—

"A cabin for the coordinator," Orion said, barely glancing at the plans. "All of our coordinators in Denver will live on-site for free. It's part of their compensation."

A surge of jealousy hit Amber, very much like the ones she'd experienced while shopping with her sister for her wedding or tasting all the divine way a professional chef could make cake delicious.

"Wow," Amber said. "Amazing." As she continued her meeting and went out to the location of the ranch in the beautiful hills of the Rocky Mountains, Amber couldn't help feeling like she needed to be here, in Colorado.

Not at Last Chance Ranch.

Chapter Nineteen

Lance sat on his front steps, his eyes on his fingers on the neck of the guitar he held. He would not look down the road again. He would not.

Amber had extended her time in Colorado by a week, and then another, and she'd promised she'd be back for the wedding.

He didn't think he'd miss one of her best friend's weddings, which was tomorrow afternoon, and she'd texted him to say she was on the plane a few hours ago. She should be pulling in any minute—but Lance would not look again.

He would not.

He plucked chords by watching his fingers as if he'd never played the guitar before. His heart had been shrinking since Amber had left, and until that morning,

Lance had started to doubt she'd ever come back to Last Chance Ranch.

The crunch of tires against the gravel brought his head up. The music coming from the instrument stalled as Amber's car came closer and closer. His heart pounded so fast and so loud, and he forced himself to move slowly as he stood and balanced his guitar against the post.

He went down the steps as she pulled into his drive-way. A squeal filled the air as she got out of the car and ran around the front of it, not even bothering to close her door.

"Lance." She laughed his name out as she flung her arms around him, and Lance couldn't help chuckling as he wrapped his arms around Amber and held on tight. She smelled like lemons and mint, and he drew in a deep breath of her, so glad she'd come home.

"I missed you so much," she said, pulling back and stretching up to kiss him. Lance's fears fled with her lips against his, and he couldn't believe he'd ever doubted her.

She sighed and fell back, glancing around the ranch as if she'd never been there before. "Ah, I missed this place."

Lance didn't like that she'd been gone so long, but all of their conversations via text and phone had told her that. He hadn't been shy about his disappointment when she hadn't come back when she'd said she would. After that, he'd kept their conversations light and easy.

She knew how he felt about her, and she'd had the ball solidly in her court for a while now. Lance didn't mind the dating. She needed time to know how she felt about him.

No problem. The time apart, the distance between them, it all proved to him how fond of her he still was.

How much he wanted her in his life permanently.

"So...." she said, a sexy little smile on her face. "Do you want to take me to lunch?"

He'd eaten a couple of hours ago, but he said, "Yes," anyway. He just wanted to spend time with her, and she'd been gone for eighteen days.

"Jump in, cowboy." She walked back toward her side of the car, and Lance folded himself into the front seat of her sedan.

"The facility in Denver is amazing," Amber said, her voice full of joy. "It's so big, and everything is brand new."

"I didn't think they were building it yet," Lance said.

"Yeah, sure they are," she said, cutting him a look out of the corner of her eye. "It opens in six months. Well, seven. So the main barns are going in, the stables, all the roads, the volunteer houses, the cabins...." She kept detailing all the plans that were happening at this new rescue ranch.

Lance tried to listen, but he had a hard time picturing the things she was talking about. Honestly, it sounded like a great place, but he knew it wouldn't have the spirit of Last Chance Ranch.

"Will anyone live on it?" he asked. "Like a real ranch?"

"I think there will be a few people who live on-site full-time," she said. "But Forever Friends owns the facility. It's not really a ranch."

"Does it have a name?"

"Triple F Ranch," she said as if that were the most clever name in the world. "It stands for Forever Friends Facility."

"Not super original," he said with a smile.

"I mean, it has a certain ring to it." Amber pulled into the fast-casual Mexican place and looked up at the doors. "They look busy, but this is exactly what I want. I've eaten so many steaks and hamburgers in Denver."

"Really?" he asked. "They don't have Mexican food there?"

"I'm sure they do, but every time the team went out, it seemed to be beef-centric."

"Cache would like that."

"How's everything going for the wedding?" she asked as they walked in.

Lance was surprised she'd even remembered there was a wedding. She hadn't been able to talk about anything but the facility or Denver in days.

"Well, seeing as how it's in twenty-four hours, I guess everything is going great," he said. "My mother's been helping with the tutus for the cows. I'm supposed to go help dress the bovines in the morning."

"And they're really wearing tutus?"

"It's what Karla wants," Lance said with a smile. "And Karla is getting everything Karla wants."

"I'll bet she is," Amber said.

Lance grinned as he stepped up to order his burrito

plate. She ordered too, and they moved down the line. Once they had their food, he led them to a booth in the corner, and as he sat across from her, he couldn't help feeling like the part of him that had been missing had been found.

"I'm so glad you're back," he said, picking up his plastic fork.

"Me, too," she said. "But there's this *amazing* place to watch the sun go down in Denver...." Amber kept talking about the red rocks and the huge Rocky Mountains, and Lance enjoyed the enthusiasm and joy in her voice.

But he couldn't help feeling like the woman he'd said good-bye to eighteen days ago was not the same woman sitting across from him.

And he had no idea what to do with that feeling.

***

THE NEXT MORNING, Lance hopped the fence to the pasture where Cache and Karla would be getting married. Cache was already there, wearing a pair of blue jeans and a blue plaid shirt that looked like it had been run over by a baler.

Ames and Cook stood nearby as well, and Sawyer joined Lance only a few seconds after he'd hopped the fence. "I can't believe we're dressing cows," he said with a shake of his head.

Liz Isaacson

"Hey," Lance said. "It's better than some weddings I've been to."

"Are you serious?" Sawyer asked. "What kind of friends do you have?"

Lance chuckled. "My sister married a guy who loves hunting. There were literally antlers *every*where." They both laughed, sobering as they approached Cache, who stood beside two cows lying on the ground. They barely looked up at the newcomers, and Lance thought he should probably give Cache's cow cuddling a shot.

"Morning," Cache said to everyone. "There are ten tutus here. We just need to get 'em on the cows." He picked up one of the frilly pink pieces of clothing. "They Velcro," he said. "But it'll probably take two people to get it on a cow. My dairy cows aren't skinny." He grinned around at everyone. "Thanks so much for coming."

"I'm with you," Lance said, stepping toward Cache.

"Cook and Ames, grab a tutu," he said. "Sawyer, you come with me and Lance."

Lance loved his bandmates, though he was about to become the only single member of Last Chance Cowboys. He lost himself inside those thoughts for a moment, only breaking out of them when Sawyer said, "Did Amber make it back?"

"Yeah," Lance said. "Yesterday afternoon. She should be here for the wedding."

"She's here," Cache said. "I saw her car parked behind Karla's house this morning."

"You've already been to her house?" Sawyer asked. "Don't you know it's bad luck to see the bride before the wedding?"

"I didn't see her dress," Cache said, rolling his eyes. "I had to pick up the tutus. Oh, there's Hudson."

The other cowboy came walking across the pasture, carrying a huge white roll of canvas over his shoulder.

"I'll help with the tent," Sawyer said, moving away from where Cache still stood next to the lazy cows.

"All right." Cache clapped his hands. "Stand up Cookie. Bluebell." Neither cow moved, and Lance looked at Cache for his next step.

"I've spent months training them to lay down," he said with a smile. "Just pull on the rope."

Lance bent and collected the rope around one of the cow's necks. He had no idea if it was Bluebell or Cookie, or even how to tell the difference. All cows looked the same to him. "Come on, girl," he said, his voice gentle. To his surprise, the cow lumbered to her feet, a bit of annoyance in her gaze.

"Great," Cache said. "Let me get this around her...." He unclasped the tutu and threw it over the cow's back. Working together, they looped the fabric around until they could press all the Velcro pieces together along the cow's back.

"There you go, Bluebell," Cache said. "You look so pretty for the wedding."

Lance felt his laughter building in the back of his

throat. Finally, he couldn't hold it in anymore, and it came pouring from his mouth, filling the sky.

Thankfully, Cache joined in. "Did I just tell a cow she looked pretty for the wedding?"

"Yes, you did," Lance said, dropping Bluebell's rope and reaching for the next one.

"This is ridiculous. I'm not wearing this shirt either."

Lance looked at him in surprise. "That's the shirt you're wearing? It looks like it lost a fight with a weed eater." He pointed to a hole on the sleeve. "It literally has holes, Cache."

"I know."

"You can't get married in that."

"Karla said she wanted me to wear this blue shirt."

Lance frowned. "Why?"

"She doesn't want things to be too fancy."

"She's wearing a dress, right?"

"Yeah, but it's not a great big fancy thing." Cache slipped another tutu around Cookie's midsection. "But I think I better wear my suit."

"Uh, yeah," Lance said. "Do you want me to see if I can get Amber to tell me a little about the dress?"

"No, I've seen it," Cache said. "It's definitely a wedding dress. It's just not miles of lace or yards of sequins."

"Then you can't wear a shirt full of holes."

"There's one hole."

"That's one too many," Lance said as they grabbed a

couple more tutus and moved toward the next cow. "I mean, it's your wedding day."

"Yeah," Cache said, growing serious. "How are you and Amber doing?"

Lance squinted into the morning sunlight and exhaled. "Okay."

"Just okay?

"Honestly? I think she's about to break up with me."

"Why do you think that?"

"I don't know," Lance said, the weight that had been in his stomach since she'd left for Denver coming back with a vengeance. "It's just how I feel."

Chapter Twenty

Amber appreciated that Karla had not gone hog wild with the bridesmaid requirements. In fact, there was no special bridesmaid dress each woman had to wear. She wanted the wedding to be more casual, more fun, more lively.

So Amber got to wear what she wanted, as long as she didn't upstage the cows. She wasn't sure how anyone could outdo a cow wearing a tutu, but she had a pale pink dress that made her eyes stand out. It had wide straps across her shoulders, and she'd swept her hair up into a knot on the top of her head.

She loved being in Karla's small cabin with her and the other women, but she felt out of place now too. Jeri, Adele, Sissy and Scarlett had brought their babies, though they lay in playpens, asleep amid the ruckus the women made.

After all, it took a lot of chatter to put on makeup and

get up-dos done, and make sure every piece of jewelry was in the proper place.

Amber felt like she was on the other side of a window, when she'd used to be inside with everyone else. She'd been gone for two and a half weeks, and she'd missed some things around the ranch. Babies grew by leaps and bounds in two and a half weeks, and motherhood or the wedding was all anyone seemed to be able to talk about.

Amber wasn't a mother. She wasn't getting married. And she didn't know when either of those would happen for her.

A feeling moved through her that she couldn't quite name, and she felt more strongly about going to Colorado permanently after Christmas. Oh, how she loved Christmas on this ranch. Scarlett decorated Prime with wreaths and bells and lights, changing his attire every few days.

She and Hudson had all the regulars to the homestead on Christmas Eve, where they'd hung a stocking for each person earlier in the months. Gifts were exchanged. Ham eaten. Prayers said.

Amber had come to the ranch just before Christmas a few years ago, and the celebration and sense of family love she'd felt at that meal had literally saved her life. How could she leave this ranch behind, even for a new facility and a better job?

What about Lance?

They'd had a fun lunch yesterday, but about halfway

through, she'd sensed him pulling away from her. True, she'd talked and talked about Denver, but when she'd stopped that, it almost seemed like they had nothing else to talk about.

Lance had never been a man of many words, and Amber hadn't worried about it. He still kissed her like he sure did like her, and she'd really missed him. He'd finally said his mother wasn't feeling well again, but that she'd be at the wedding tomorrow.

Amber had said nothing about her possible move to Denver. She had a feeling Jewel had asked her to go to the facility and sit in on the meetings in the hopes that Amber would feel exactly the way she did—that she'd want to be part of the good things happening at this new place.

And she did.

But she wanted Lance too.

She pulled up short at the thought. Yes, she liked Lance, and she enjoyed spending time with him. But she'd literally never had a man she actually wanted to be with long-term. The very idea scared her, and she turned toward Adele and asked, "How did you decide to come back to Last Chance Ranch after you'd gone to New York?"

Adele blinked a few times, obviously not expecting the question. Amber wasn't even sure where it had come from.

"I came back for Scarlett's wedding," she said, recovering nicely and turning back to the mirror on the counter in front of her. "And Carson did too, and it was just...

magic." She shrugged, her dress a bright blue that made her hair look blonder and her freckles stand out. "I knew then that a restaurant job wasn't more important than him."

"But you did go to New York in the first place," Amber said.

"Sure," Adele said. "It had been a dream of mine for years and years." She teased up one last piece of hair. "And I wouldn't have become the person I am today without that experience. It was hard in a lot of ways, but I learned a lot too."

"Adele," Scarlett said. "James spit up a little."

Adele got right up and hurried over to the playpen where her baby had been sleeping with one of Scarlett's. Amber watched them coo to and cuddle their babies, an extreme pang of longing ripping through her.

She did want to be a mother.

Her phone rang, startling her from her stare-fest. "Hey, JJ," she said after she'd opened the call. "What's up?"

"You'll never believe what's happened," her sister said. She didn't even wait for Amber to ask what before she continued. "The venue made a mistake. They double-booked us with another couple, and they booked first, and now I can't have the date I want."

Amber closed her eyes and prayed for patience. "I'm sorry, Jay. What are you going to do?"

"They can put me on the twenty-seventh."

Amber waited, because she wasn't sure what month her sister was talking about. "What day of the week is that?" she asked when JJ remained silent. "Isn't Thanksgiving near there?"

"Of December." JJ started crying softly. "I don't want to get married at Christmas," she said.

Amber didn't see why not, but she said, "Oh, December," as if it were the worst month to get married. Maybe in Montana or Maine, but December in California was nothing to cry over. Usually.

"That's like six weeks later," Amber said.

"It's all they have," JJ said. "So I either book that, or I find somewhere else. And you know everywhere good is going to be booked too."

Amber didn't know that, but she hadn't spent much time thinking about or planning her wedding.

"Then book it, JJ," Amber said, letting a little of her impatience seep into her voice. "You love that reception center, and so what if it's near Christmas? It's really three-hundred-and-sixty-three days *away* from Christmas."

"Will you come if it's at Christmas?"

"Why wouldn't I?"

"I don't know. I thought you'd be in Denver by then."

"I'm not moving to Denver permanently," Amber said, slip of misery moving through her. "I mean, I might be there, but of course I'll come back for the wedding."

Her sister sniffled through a few more details, and Amber hung up.

"You might be in Denver at Christmas?"

Amber looked up at Scarlett, who had a baby over one shoulder, swaying as she swatted his bottom.

"I mean, maybe," Amber said evasively.

"Why?"

Amber looked at her boss, her friend. "Forever Friends has offered me a big promotion at a facility in Denver that's opening soon."

Scarlett's eyes widened. "Oh."

"Yeah," Amber said, fully miserable now. "Oh." Before she could say more, Karla came out of the back bedroom with her sister and mother flanking her, and a general cry went up, stealing Scarlett's attention.

Amber rode the interruption, because she didn't want to talk about the job. Or Lance. Or anything about herself. She oohed and aahed with the other women, and she hugged Karla tight in her very simple wedding dress.

It dipped and fell in all the right places, but it wasn't huge, or frilly, or immaculate with bead work or sequins. Somehow it was exactly what Karla should wear to her wedding on the ranch, and soon enough, someone opened the front door with the words, "We better get over to the pasture, or we'll all be late."

Amber went with them, once again noticing that she didn't have anyone to walk with. Karla had her family here. The other women had babies and families and new worries in their lives. They probably weren't sleeping through the night.

But Amber was, and she also couldn't help wondering how she was going to tell Lance she might want the job after all.

A big tent had been set up in the pasture across the street from the homestead, and all the cows wore bright pink tutus. There seemed to be some excitement over that, and many of the wedding guests were getting their pictures taken with the dairy cows. Amber wanted one too, and she had Gina, the large animal vet, take one for her on her cell phone.

The bell at the homestead started ringing, the same way it did for all special occasions here on the ranch. People started filing into their seats from various places around the ranch, and it seemed like there would be guests wearing plaid shirts and jeans, their work gloves stuck in their back pockets.

Lance better be wearing something nicer than that, and she looked around for him. He stood with the rest of the men in Last Chance Cowboys, a guitar in his hands that he handed to Cache a moment later.

He positioned himself behind the drums, and a slow wedding march started to play. They went through it several times before the wedding party assembled, and then Carson and Adele led the way down the aisle to the temporary altar that had been erected.

Amber walked down the aisle with a bouquet of wild-flowers in her hands, Sissy and baby Evelyn as her partners. Once everyone was in place, the band finished up, and the members came down to their spots in the wedding.

Cache glowed like the Northern Lights, and he swept a kiss across Karla's cheek, pausing to whisper something in her ear before Pastor Williams began talking.

"What a lovely occasion," he said. "Weddings are such great events to feel the love of the Lord. Funerals too. Anything that brings us together and reminds us of those we love, and that love us."

He paused to smile at Karla and Cache. "Now, I want to give a word of advice to the happy couple today before we get the job done. And it's this—don't be afraid to talk to one another. Rely on each other and God before other people. And you can't do that if you aren't communicating." He nodded at Cache, who nodded back. "Pray together. Pray separately. Confide in each other your fears, struggles, joys, and triumphs, and you'll be blessed."

Amber smiled at her friends, her heart full and her spirit singing. What Pastor Williams had said was absolutely true. She'd wanted someone to confide in for a very long time, and Lance was the first man she'd had in her life where she felt safe doing so.

She looked at him through her tears, unsure as to why her heart was beating so erratically. She didn't hear the rest of the nuptials, only realizing things were over when a cheer went up. She blinked, a tear running down her perfectly made up face, and saw Cache and Karla kissing.

When they broke apart, they looked absolutely joyful, and Amber wanted that feeling in her life too.

The moment she could, she navigated over to Lance and slipped her arm through his. "Hey," she said. "I need to talk to you."

"What's wrong?" he asked, peering down into her face.

"I don't know how to say this." But she needed to say it. She wanted to confide in him. Talk to him. "But I think I should take that job in Denver."

Chapter Twenty-One

I *think I should take that job in Denver.* The words taunted him for the rest of the wedding. All night long. Through the next day. Forever. They'd haunt him forever, especially the ones he'd said right after Amber's.

Then you should take it.

He said the words under his breath as he locked up enclosure eight for the day. Amber hadn't broken up with him, but if she was really going to take that job in Denver, she might as well say good-bye now.

It would probably be less painful for both of them. Sure, they'd been dating for six months, which was a very long time for her. For him, too, truth be told. He was already in love with her, and what would six more months do?

Torture him, that was what six more months would do.

Show him a life he couldn't have. One that would be ripped away from him right after the holidays.

Determined now, he kept his pace brisk as he walked toward the volunteer house. The cross-country team was coming for the last time to get the dogs for their combined run, so Amber would be outside with everyone.

Sure enough, she was, her curls hanging over her shoulders in delicious waves. Lance's fingers curled into a fist, and he arrived just as the volunteers from the Canine Club did, bringing dogs with them.

Everyone got the rules again, and the leashes were passed out. The runners left with the dogs, and Lance ducked into the volunteer house, where there'd at least be air conditioning.

Amber entered a few seconds later, and she stilled when she saw Lance. Fear danced across her face, but she said, "Hey, cowboy," as if nothing between them had changed.

But it had.

Lance had changed too, and so had Amber. He didn't smile back at her or act like everything was okay.

"I think we should stop seeing each other," he said, his voice barely leaving his throat. He tried to clear the emotion from it, only creating a loud noise that made him flinch.

Amber just looked at him resolutely. "I think you should come with me to Denver."

He started shaking his head before she'd even finished

talking. "My family is here, Amber. My mother needs my help."

"She can come too."

"What's she going to do in Denver?"

"What does she do here?" she challenged.

Lance felt the wind go out of his sails. He didn't want to fight with this woman. He didn't want to say something he couldn't take back later. "Amber, I...I think you should take the job if you feel good about it. I'm not going to stop you from doing that."

She nodded, letting her gaze roam around the room.

"But I don't think I can keep dating you, only to know you'll leave in six months." He took his cowboy hat off, wiped his hand through his hair, and reseated his hat. "Seems better to just end things here. I'm sorry." He nodded one final time and headed for the door, giving her a wide berth.

He had his hand on the doorknob when she said, "What if I don't want to break up?"

"You do," he said. "Or the job wouldn't even be an option." He opened the door and stepped outside, the air out here so much easier to breathe when it wasn't full of her perfume, the fruity candles she burned, her very essence.

"Lance," she said, and he stalled at the top of the few steps, a sigh working through him. "I don't want to break up."

"Amber," he said, turning back to her. She'd moved

closer to him, and he could reach out and take her into his arms if he wanted to. And oh, he wanted to. "How long have you been here on the ranch?"

"Two and a half years," she said.

"How long is the longest assignment you've had for Forever Friends?"

A line appeared between her eyes as she frowned. "I— don't know. Probably this one."

Exactly what he thought. "I already know you've dated me the longest out of anyone in a long time," he said. "And I think you just have a gypsy spirit. If it's not Denver, something else will call to you soon enough, and you'll chase after that." He tried to smile, but it hurt so much. "Maybe you're just not one to be tied down, to anyone or any place. And that's fine."

"It's not fine," she said, her voice tinny and high.

He didn't want to make her cry, but he felt dangerously close to losing his control too. "I'll see you later." He went down the steps and on down the road, never looking back. If he did, he was sure he'd run back to her, take everything back he'd said, and beg her to let him be her boyfriend again. Even for one more day.

But deep down, he knew he didn't want that. He wanted the type of love that bridged everything. That brought people closer, that spanned time and space and eternity.

And Amber Haws had never committed to anything for longer than two and a half years. He made it all the way back to his cabin, both dogs vying for his attention, before he drew a full breath again.

That was hard, and he wondered if he'd ever be able to breathe normally without Amber in his life.

HE MADE it through the next day, and then the next, and then a week. He went over to his mother's in the evening, choosing to be with someone rather than being alone. She didn't mind if he brought his dogs, because they didn't weigh over a hundred pounds and remind her of her husband. In fact, she'd really taken to Maddie, and Lance was considering asking his mom if she wanted the little lap dog for herself.

She was great company during the day, and Lance was never home at that time. He'd be fine with Ribbon, and so he offered.

"You want to give me your dog?" His mom stopped her crocheting, something that rarely happened. "Why? What's going on?"

"Nothing's going on, Mom," Lance said, regretting the offer. "I just thought you liked her, and look at her. She's all cuddled up to you while you knit."

"It's crochet," she said. "And I'm not taking your dog."

"But you like this one, and she could keep you company during the day."

"Oh, James keeps me company. Or Scarlett lets me

hold those babies." She picked up her stitch again and peered at him at the same time. How she could do that without looking, he didn't know. "So what happened? This isn't about me being lonely."

"So you are lonely." He sat down in the recliner he liked best and leaned back, a long sigh coming from his mouth. "I'm tired."

"I'll admit I'm a little bit lonely, but being here is about ten times better than being alone in that house."

Lance heard the undercurrent of emotion in his mother's voice. "And yet, you weren't very open to leaving that house the first time I suggested it."

"I just needed time."

"So think about taking Maddie off my hands," he said. "Honestly, I think she'd be happier. Ribbon would be. And so would you."

"Where does that leave you?"

"About where I always am," he said.

"Lance."

He let his eyes drift closed, because he was tired. Oh, so tired. Just plain exhausted from all the physical work he did around the ranch, to the emotional toll of not being able to text Amber had extracted from him.

"Where's Amber tonight?" she asked, and he gave a soft snore as if he'd fallen asleep. "Oh, you silly man," his mother said. "I know you're not asleep. Fine, we won't talk about Amber."

"Good," Lance said. "Because I broke up with her, and

I don't want to talk about it."

"You broke up?" The level of distress in his mother's voice caused him to open his eyes and look at her. "Why?"

"I just said I didn't want to talk about it."

"I'm calling Kristen."

"What's she going to do?" Lance's heart pulsed irregularly for some reason. His sister lived an hour from the ranch, and she barely knew Amber. Kristen could literally do nothing for Lance in this situation except embarrass him.

His mom didn't answer, but she actually set aside her crocheting and reached for her phone. Lance got up though every cell in his body wanted him to stay put, take a little nap, see if his mom would feed him later.

"I'm leaving," he said. "Come on, guys."

Ribbon came, but Maddie just looked at him from the warmth of his mom's side. "Maddie's staying with you." And with that, he walked out of his mom's cabin, her last words—"Kristen, you will not believe what happened"—ringing in his ears.

He couldn't even believe what had happened. *He'd* broken up with Amber, a woman he'd liked for two years.

"Better now than at Christmas," he told himself as he walked home, Ribbon limping along beside him. Then the holiday wouldn't hold such bitter memories, and he might have a shot at moving on.

Cache came out of his cabin, laughter riding the air with him. Karla followed, each of them carrying a box, as they'd been slowly moving Cache's things over to Karla's cabin. They'd taken a quick honeymoon to Yosemite National Park, but they'd returned yesterday.

Lance watched them laugh, their love like a scent on the air. Cache pulled Karla to him and kissed her, and Lance knew then that he'd never be whole without Amber.

He'd never be able to truly move on. Not really. Not ever.

Helplessness filled him as he climbed the steps and waited for Ribbon to hobble up after him. He'd felt like this for so long when it came to Amber, and he was tired of it.

"Lord," he said as he went inside his cabin. "Help me understand why I've let this woman have such a hold over my heart for so long."

But God didn't seem too keen on granting Lance's request, because another week passed where all his thoughts centered on Amber, and then another.

The Sunday after the Fourth of July, he sat in the chapel, listening to the choir sing. The angels in heaven seemed to be in attendance, as he heard more voices than there were bodies up on the dais. He'd come very early to church today, because he was still searching for the answers he needed in his life.

What should I do differently? he prayed. *Help me see the right path. Give me courage to take the first step.*

But he couldn't see. Couldn't feel. Couldn't step.

Chapter Twenty-Two

A mber rubbed her eyes as she waited for Jewel to call her back into her office. She hated coming to Los Angeles to the Forever Friends headquarters, but paperwork needed to be signed, and Jewel couldn't get out of the office.

So Amber had made the drive into the city, leaving Last Chance Ranch in the hands of Susanna Rodriguez, the woman Amber was training to take her place as the volunteer coordinator and adoption specialist.

Things had been moving faster than she'd anticipated, and she'd be in Denver by mid-August. It was too close and yet too far away at the same time. She couldn't help looking to her left every time she drove onto the ranch. Lance lived down that first road, and she wanted to catch a glimpse of him.

She never did. They'd worked together a lot over the

past couple of years, even before he'd shown up with the doughnuts and upended her existence. But he seemed to have completely disappeared the past few weeks, and Amber didn't blame him.

She wouldn't want to be around someone like her. She'd spoken true that she didn't want to break up, but Lance was also right. She hadn't ever committed to anything—a man, a job, even a pet—for longer than a couple of years. Theirs was the longest relationship she'd been in, and this assignment for Forever Friends was the one she'd had for the longest time.

Heck, even Cyclops, her rescue cat, had only been with her for eighteen months.

"Amber, she's ready for you." Janice smiled at Amber as she stood, and Amber tried to wipe the emotion and exhaustion from her face before she entered Jewel's office.

"Hello, dear," Jewel said, not bothering to look up from her desk. "Sorry to make you wait. We had an incident out on the farm in Portland that I needed to check on." She glanced up, a smile on her face. Their eyes met, and Jewel abandoned whatever she'd been working on. "You still want to do this, right?"

"Yes," Amber said. She'd been praying about it and praying about it, and everything felt so right. She'd been on conference calls with the team in Denver, and she liked them. She enjoyed giving her opinion and having it listened to. She felt valued there, and appreciated, and stretched.

That was the biggest one. She loved Last Chance Ranch. Loved her friends there, loved the work, and she knew she was important and valuable to the operation. But everything had become stale there. Even training the goats for yoga didn't hold the same spark it once had.

She couldn't help thinking of what Lance had said. *You just have a gypsy spirit.*

So she'd go to Denver and get the new facility up and running. Train a half a dozen people to do what she did. And then what?

That question had been plaguing her for weeks. *Then what?*

She couldn't answer it. God didn't, no matter how many times she asked.

She reminded herself that she was loved. She'd felt that, and she couldn't deny it. She also knew going to Colorado was the right thing, so there was no way she could doubt those feelings and promptings. She just didn't understand why she had to sacrifice Lance—one of the best things that had ever happened to her—to fulfill her "gypsy spirit."

Jewel laid out all the paperwork, though Amber had seen it all before. They'd been in constant contact over the project in Denver. She signed everything, hugged Jewel, and left the huge office building that had a doggy daycare on the bottom floor, as well as an animal hospital where they trained dogs and cats before they went out to homes. The second floor was dedicated to the rehabilitation of animals they found on the street, or animals born with genetic defects or life-threatening conditions.

Amber loved the work Forever Friends did, and she sent up a prayer of gratitude that she had a job she loved.

But had she had to give up a man she loved in order to keep the job?

AN HOUR LATER, she slid into the booth opposite her sister. Her mom moved over to make more room for her, saying, "There you are. We were just about to call you."

"Sorry," she said. "There was an accident, and traffic is snarled right now."

"Already?" JJ asked, looking out the window as if she'd be able to see the freeway from here. She scowled and reached for her diet cola.

Amber didn't particularly enjoy spending time with her family, but she'd asked her mom and sister to a late lunch in the city, as they were there looking at stationery and seals for the upcoming wedding.

"I have some news," she said, looking up at the waiter as he arrived.

"Drinks?"

"Yes, I'll have a peach lemonade."

He nodded and left, and Amber faced her mom again. "You're engaged to that cowboy." Her mother shrieked, drawing the attention of everyone within a ten-table radius.

"Mom," Amber hissed. "No."

Neither of them seemed to hear her. "I told you, Mom." JJ glared at Amber—actually *glared* at her. "You can't get married until at least a year after me. I get a year."

Amber stared at her, dumbfounded. "You need a year...to do what?"

"Mom," JJ whined. "Now I'm not going to be able to get everything I want."

"Of course you will," her mother said.

"Not if Amber's engaged too. My wedding isn't for six more months. I can't have your attention be divided."

"I'm not engaged," Amber said, glaring at her sister now. She'd always gotten the lion's share of their mother's attention. Always. When they were younger, JJ was constantly sick. Constantly at the doctor. Constantly calling their mom to come get her from school. And her mother did it. Took her to lunch. Bought her the soups she wanted. All the ice cream. Everything.

"It will be fine," her mom said. "I'm sure Amber will get married on the ranch like all her other friends. It'll be so much simpler than yours." She said it as if simple was bad. As if getting married at Last Chance Ranch was the worst move anyone could possibly make.

"I'm not engaged," Amber said again, more forcefully this time.

JJ had opened her mouth to say something, but she switched her gaze to Amber instead. "What?"

"I'm not engaged," she practically growled this time. "I got a big promotion at work. That's the news."

The waiter set her peach lemonade down and said, "Do you ladies need a few more minutes?" He knocked on the table. "I'm going to give you a few more minutes."

The silence that followed his departure grated against Amber's nerves. She reached for the straw and unwrapped it before sticking it in her drink. She needed to cool off before she said anything else.

"A promotion," her mom said. "That's great, sweetie."

"Is it?" Amber asked. "Because you sound like I just told you I'd been fired." She shook her head, even the sweetly sour taste of the lemonade not working to soothe her. "In fact, I broke up with Lance. Or rather, he broke up with me." She bit back the wave of sadness that threatened to drown her. Every time she thought of him she had to brace herself against this tide. "And I'm leaving California. I'm moving to Denver in four weeks."

She scooted to the end of the bench and got out of the booth. "Thanks for the lemonade." She opened her purse and pulled out a five-dollar bill. "I have to go."

"Amber," JJ said, but Amber just glared her into silence.

"You invited us to lunch," her mother reminded her.

"Yeah," Amber said. "I don't know what I was thinking. Enjoy yourselves." She walked away, her head high but her heart sinking, sinking, sinking to the soles of her shoes. Her fingers shook as she walked out of the cool restaurant and into the heat. Behind the wheel of her car, tears filled her eyes.

She only had one person she wanted to call and talk to, explain everything that had just happened, and find comfort in.

Lance.

And she certainly couldn't do that, not when she'd chosen a job over him.

AMBER TALKED TO EDITH, McKenna, and Diane about taking Cyclops, but none of her friends wanted a declawed, blind cat. She couldn't bear to put him back in Feline Frenzy, because if those who cared about her wouldn't take him, she didn't think anyone would.

Lance had two rescue cats, and he'd liked Cyclops well enough, but she couldn't ask him. She hadn't spoken to him in weeks, and as the day approached that she'd be leaving Last Chance Ranch for good, the need to see him one last time started seething.

But she would not call him and ask him to take her blind cat so she could move three states over and start a new job. She would not. Talk about rubbing salt in an open wound. Just hearing his voice would undo all the decisions she'd made over the past month.

"Well, let me know if you change your mind," she said to McKenna. The goat yoga instructor waved as she left, and Amber looked up when the door didn't close when it should've.

Lance's mother stood there.

Amber jumped to her feet. "Jamie Lee."

"Did you think you could leave this ranch without saying good-bye to me?" She looked stern, but in the next moment, a smile broke out across her face.

Amber half-sobbed and half-laughed as she crossed the volunteer house to hug Lance's mother. "Of course not," she said as she felt the motherly embrace she'd longed for. "I just wasn't sure if you'd want to see me."

"I'll admit I was a little upset with you when I found out you were leaving."

Amber pulled back. "Not upset about me and Lance?"

"Oh, he's upset about that for the both of us." Jamie Lee wiped her eyes. "Though I did think—do think—you two are absolutely perfect for each other."

Amber turned away, not wanting to cry in front of his mom. She'd been keeping things together one hour at a time. One good-bye at a time. Scarlett had planned a going away party for her, but it wasn't for another couple of days, as Amber wasn't leaving until Saturday.

"I sure do like him," she said.

"Maybe ask him to go with you," Jamie Lee suggested.

"I did."

"You did?"

"Yes. I said you should come too, because he doesn't want to leave you here by yourself."

She blinked, her eyes widening with each one. "He said that?"

Amber realized she'd made a mistake. "I mean...he loves you. You're his mother, and he feels responsible for you." She picked up a candle she'd bought for Jamie Lee. "I got this for you. You've been so wonderful to me, and I'm going to miss you." Her voice cracked on the last two words, but she held onto her composure as she passed the gift to Jamie Lee.

She unwrapped the box, sniffling as she did. "Oh, it's the frosted peach you've told me about." She looked up, her eyes so bright and so full of life. "Thank you, Amber."

Amber simply hugged her again, because she didn't trust herself to speak.

"Good luck to you," she said. "Don't be a stranger. I sit around with my phone all day, you know." She smiled with watery eyes and turned toward the door. As she left, Amber heard her say, "I'm going to go talk to my son."

Chapter Twenty-Three

Lance barely looked up from his grilled cheese sandwich when his mother walked into his cabin. She carried something in her hands, but he knew why she was there. After all, she'd called and had been lecturing him for the full fifteen minutes it took her to walk from the volunteer house to his cabin.

"I can't believe you," she said.

"You said that already," he deadpanned. Amber had ratted him out. Unknowingly, of course. But still. "Mom, I don't want to move to Denver. You don't want to go to Denver either." He put the last bite of his dinner in his mouth and stood up to put his plate in the sink.

"Why wouldn't I want to go to Denver?" she asked in a self-righteous tone that made Lance roll his eyes.

He swallowed and leaned against the counter, facing her. "Mom, you wouldn't be able to go see Dad's grave.

Number two, you wouldn't see those grandkids you're always bragging about. Three, you hate the snow. Should I go on?" He cocked his eyebrows at her, annoyed at the conversation but glad he was having one.

He'd taken to staying in during the evenings, as all anyone wanted to talk about was their family, their new wife, or why he and Amber had broken up. He'd seen all these other men and women get their last chance at happiness, and dang if he didn't want his.

The jealous feelings had been sticking around longer and longer, and Lance couldn't seem to fight them off as quickly as he once had. He didn't like the bad feelings he had for his friends, the people around the ranch he'd grown to love and trust. The reason he loved this ranch so much was because of those relationships, and the spirit he felt here.

"I would go," his mom said. "Because you should go, and you're right. I don't want to be on this ranch by myself. But you can't let her leave."

"I can," Lance said. "I haven't even spoken to her in a couple of months. I'm doing okay."

"You are not," his mom said. "You haven't gone to any of the church activities, and you take on more work than you should."

"I'm fine, Mom. The ranch is a busy place. Someone has to do the work." He turned to the fridge and pulled out a bottle of water. "You want something to drink?"

"I want you to go make up with that woman."

Lance uncapped the water and took a long, long drink. The chill burned his throat, and still he drank. He couldn't look away from his mother either. He didn't want to say anything bad against Amber. But his mother deserved to know the truth. Maybe then she'd get off his back about this break up.

"Mom," he said calmly after draining the whole bottle of water. "*She* chose something else over me, okay? *She's* the one who did that. Not me. *She* chose Denver. *She* chose the promotion. *She chose* to leave." His chest heaved, and he felt like he'd been transported back fifteen years, to when Peggy had done the same thing.

Women always chose something else over Lance, and he wasn't sure why.

He felt so inadequate. So lost. He sighed, and said, "Sorry, Mom. I'm taking Ribbon for a walk." It was much too hot for such things, and Lance just wanted to stay in the air-conditioned cabin, kick off his boots, and eat an ice cream bar.

But he grabbed a leash he wouldn't use and said, "Let's go, Rib."

Outside, he didn't feel quite so lost, as God had anchored him to this place. "Am I enough for you, Lord?"

The sweetest sense of reassurance came over him, and Lance finally relaxed for the first time since he'd walked away from the volunteer house. He'd been sending others to deal with any adoptions or the other things he used to take on himself, just so he'd have a reason to see Amber.

It had been surprisingly easy to avoid her, but of course he knew she was leaving Last Chance Ranch on Saturday. It was all anyone, anywhere, could talk about.

He knew Scarlett was throwing Amber a party on Friday night, because all the men had asked if they could come to his house after band practice. Even Carson and Hudson, who weren't in the band. Ames, too.

Lance had said he wouldn't be in the partying mood, but Cache and Cook had insisted they bring pizza and soda and "try to distract" him.

He scoffed as he wandered around the U-shaped Cabin Community, his dog limping alongside him. He felt so much like Ribbon, like Amber had cut him off at the legs but he was still trying to walk.

He'd tried several "distractions" over the past couple of months, and none of them had worked. His knees hurt from the attempts at running with the cross-country team. His back hurt from his attempts to squeeze more work into his already full day. And his heart hurt from his attempt at signing up for ChristianCatch, a dating app Dave had told him about.

Nothing had worked, and Lance didn't know where to turn or what to do next.

Maybe you should go to Denver streamed through his mind again. The thought had been present and persistent for weeks now, but he'd never encouraged it. Never allowed it room to grow. He couldn't. It was simply too dangerous, and there were so many roadblocks between the thought and reality.

His mother, for one.

As if summoned by his thoughts, she texted him just two words. *I'm sorry.* Lance's chest pinched, and he looked up into the cloudless California sky, a single plea for the Lord now.

"Make the pain bearable."

HOURS MARCHED ON, and days passed. He entertained his friends on Friday night, though his heart wasn't in it. Lance's heart wasn't in a whole lot of anything, and everyone around him knew it.

Saturday morning, he sat on the back steps, throwing a little ball for Maddie, who only brought it back one out of every three throws. Amber was leaving today. He imagined her little red brick house all packed up, neighbors and friends coming to help load the truck, her getting behind the wheel and facing the long drive ahead.

He wanted to be there so badly. But he couldn't get himself up to go. She didn't want him there, and that was what really mattered.

About ten o'clock, his mother arrived, a large soda cup in her hand. She gave it to him without a word and sat beside him on the steps.

"You went to town," he said, taking a long draw of the

drink. The lemon she'd put in the Diet Coke tasted great, and he felt refreshed from what was sure to be an oppressively hot day.

"Yes."

He knew why, so he didn't ask. Just bent to pick up the ball when Maddie finally brought it back and tossed it for her again. Ribbon wobbled after it, but he never picked it up, always letting the little dog get it and bring it back.

"She said good-bye, for what it's worth," his mom said. "Said she missed you and would love to talk to you."

"I'm not calling her." Besides, phone lines went both ways, and she had his number. Had never used it.

His mom patted his thigh and pushed herself up. "I know you won't. And I don't think you should. I told her I'd tell you, and I told you." She walked away, pulling her jacket around her as if she could possibly be cold in this August heat.

Lance watched her go, his chest collapsing with each passing breath. This wasn't healthy. He had to find a way to move on, but he knew better than most that a break-up was never even. And no matter who he dated, he always seemed to end up with less than half a heart, the pieces he did have left shattered beyond recognition.

Dave joined him next, surprising as the cowboy didn't even live on the ranch anymore. "Hey, man," he said. "Just checking on you."

Lance didn't want to lie, so he didn't say he was fine. The dogs had laid down an hour ago, finding a patch of shade under the steps where he sat. He didn't want to go back inside, as he didn't have anything to do there. He had no work on the ranch today, as Saturdays brought many volunteers out to work in the Canine Club.

"Thanks," he finally said to Dave. He'd watched his friend go through a hard time with Sissy too, but it had lasted a couple of days. Then she'd come back to the ranch, back to Dave, and they'd been married a month later.

The familiar jealousy coated Lance's mouth, and he reached for his drink only to find he'd finished it.

"Come to dinner tonight," he said. "Sissy makes this great sausage and potato casserole."

"Maybe," Lance said. Dave clapped him on the shoulder and left, and Lance finally got up and went inside.

The dogs jumped up on the couch and promptly fell asleep, leaving Lance with two rescue cats for company. He hadn't heard what Amber had done with Cyclops, and he hoped she'd found a good home for the cat.

Why he cared, he didn't know.

OVER THE NEXT FEW MONTHS, Lance said "Maybe," a lot. He didn't follow through on hardly any of the maybes, though, but his friends didn't stop inviting him to things.

Dinners, birthday parties, festivals, lunches, the whole nine yards.

He was grateful for such attentive friends who never allowed him to feel alone or like he was intruding on their lives.

The day after Thanksgiving, he showed up at the homestead, just like Scarlett had asked him to. "Decorating day," she said brightly, a smile on her face.

Lance loved the Christmas traditions at Lance Chance Ranch, so he grinned too. "I get to do Prime, right?"

"And all the fences," she said, as if putting lights and wreaths on hundreds of yards of fences should excite Lance.

At this moment in his life, it did.

"Everything's in the garage," she said. "Hudson's been pulling it out for a week."

Lance tipped his hat and looked to the garage as it opened. "I'll take care of it, Scarlett," he said as a baby wailed inside.

"Thanks, Lance." She dashed back inside as he walked away.

"Hey, Hudson." Lance thought he looked exhausted— much the way Lance felt. "I'll get the stuff out. You don't need to do it."

Relief crossed Hudson's face. "Miles has been sick for a week, and no one is sleeping. Well, he does, sometimes." He smiled and turned away from the bins and boxes and tall, plastic covered trees.

"I'll take care of it," Lance said as Cook arrived. He'd been around for a couple of Christmases now, and he knew what to do. He got Cook decorating the homestead with lights, and he sent Ames across the street with big, red bows to tie to the posts bordering the cow pasture where Cache and Karla had gotten married.

He said, "When you finish here, Cook, this tree goes over next to the goat yoga sign." He pointed to the covered tree. "It anchors to the ground with the kit beside it. You'll figure it out."

"I'm sure I will." Cook grinned at him and opened another box, this one with a huge light-up star on it. "This goes...where?"

"The chimney," Lance said. "Ladder's in the back there. I'm taking a bunch of stuff down to the entrance, and I'll be working there for a while." He started putting wreaths and ornaments in the back of his truck. Several boxes of lights went in too, and Lance told his dogs to move back.

When he had everything, he went down to the entrance and got to work. Stringing lights just-so around the fence wasn't fast, but it wasn't hard either. The work allowed his mind to wander, and he thought about his Lord and Savior, the one who'd been by him all these months on the ranch alone.

He'd never truly been alone, and he knew that now. He hummed a hymn as he worked, hanging ornaments on all of Prime's limbs and putting a big wreath right over his mailbox chest. He was also exactly enough for God, and he'd been looking forward to celebrating the birth of the Savior for a while now, because he knew only the Lord could truly heal him.

And he was so ready for that.

Chapter Twenty-Four

Amber had been in Denver for four months. The changing of the seasons had been magical, but that was about the only thing she could put in the pro column. It seemed like everything that could go wrong, had done exactly that.

She'd blown a tire on the way here, and thousands of dollars and five days later, she'd limped into town tired, hungry, and broke.

Forever Friends had paid for the move, but it had taken weeks to get reimbursed for the travel expenses—including the tire and the loss of some of her belongings that had been damaged in the resulting accident.

The apartment she was supposed to be able to rent had been suddenly unavailable, and she'd spent a week in a hotel while she tried to find somewhere else that wasn't an hour's commute and tried to start her new job out of a construction trailer.

She'd cried most nights, wondering why God had communicated to her that moving was so right when everything was so wrong.

Not only that, but there were no women at work anymore. Only the construction crew, which was comprised of all males, at least until all the hiring for the new facility was finished and they started training before opening in January.

She'd been asked out twice, and she'd said no both times. She was so proud of herself too, as she normally flitted from man to man, looking for any reason not to be alone. That part of her life was still a work in progress, as she didn't really like being by herself. But she also didn't want to go out with anyone but Lance.

He hadn't called or texted, though his mother had surely delivered Amber's message. It was unfair of her to expect him to, and Amber had typed out a dozen texts to him when things had fallen apart. She hadn't sent any of them, saving them all in her notes app just so she could read over them in her quiet moments, think about what Lance might've sent in return.

She'd spent Thanksgiving with a small group of people from the church she'd been attending, but she was returning to California for the first time since leaving in order to attend her sister's wedding.

There had been very little communication from her

family since that day in Los Angeles when she'd left her mother and sister at the restaurant. Amber's guilt trickled through her as a steady clip, the way it had been her whole life.

She didn't know how to get rid of it. Didn't know how to forgive the people who should've been the easiest to forgive. Didn't know why she couldn't have had a mother and siblings like Lance's. Didn't understand why God had led her to Denver only for her to find disappointment lurking around every corner.

"Stop it," she told herself as she folded her laundry so she could pack for the trip. Feeling sorry for herself had never served her well, and she needed to stitch a smile onto her face and get through this wedding.

Then, she could return to Colorado, get the new facility open, and everything would be better.

Please let that be true, she prayed as she folded a pair of jeans and put them in her suitcase. She'd be in California for a week, and that was plenty of time to help with the final preparations for the wedding, support her sister, and maybe go see her friends at Last Chance Ranch.

As he always did, Lance entered her mind, and she wondered what he'd be doing for the holiday. Now that his mother lived at the ranch, would he be there too? Maybe Arthur would host the Christmas festivities at his house. Amber could find out. She'd texted with Lance's sister a couple of times since moving, and Kristen would tell her.

Her eyes migrated from her packing to her phone,

sitting there innocently on the bed. Texting was easy. A few quick taps and done. Her resolve shifted, and she finished packing. Finished making sure the thermostat was set so things didn't freeze while she was gone.

Outside, the snow fell as she drove to the airport, making her mood surlier than it already was. But she made it onto her plane, and they were able to take off, even if the plane did shake like the devil himself wanted to bring it down.

She managed to sleep on the flight to California, and when she deplaned to sunshine, albeit weak, winter sunshine, her soul felt rejuvenated. Pausing right there in the thick traffic in the airport, she wondered what that feeling meant.

Should she move back to California?

She couldn't make huge life decisions based on current weather conditions, and she re-centered herself as she rented a car and started driving. She'd need all the focus she could get to make it through the next couple of days.

After pulling up to the house where she'd grown up, Amber simply looked out the windshield at the few cars already parked in the driveway, the yard, the building, the perfectly placed wreath on the front door. No one came to greet her, and as the moments ticked by, Amber prayed for a way to find relief from her negative thoughts about her family.

"Help me forgive them," she whispered, letting her

eyes drift closed. "There has to be a way for us to get along."

Be kind.

The words entered her mind, part of a sermon the pastor in Colorado Springs had given several weeks ago. Amber had been trying to be kinder. To the construction crew. To Jewel, who wanted long conference calls seemingly every other day. To herself.

All of that was still something she was working on too, and a heaviness filled her that she had to try again with her family.

But she would. She could, and she got out of the car and hefted her suitcase from the trunk. "Hello?" she called as she entered the house.

Chatter and music filled the house, and it actually created a vibrant, happy atmosphere that didn't seem like her family at all. Maybe she'd entered the wrong house. But no, the Haws family picture hung on the wall to her left, and her dad came out of the kitchen a moment later.

"There's my girl." He smiled at her, and Amber dropped her suitcase to hug her father.

"Hey, Daddy," she said, taking in a deep breath of him.

"Flight okay?" he asked, stepping back. "I heard there was a lot of snow in Denver."

"There is," she said with a sigh. "But my flight wasn't cancelled."

"Well, c'mon in. JJ is dying for you to meet her fiancé."

"Soon to be husband," she reminded their dad.

"Don't I know it," he said dryly. "His parents are here too."

Amber nodded, understanding the code. *Be kind. Get along.* Her mother would be mortified if Amber caused a scene, and she determined that she absolutely would not. This party would last a couple of hours, and she could do anything for that long.

Around the corner, she found JJ wearing a cute red and white party dress, almost like she wanted to be a candy cane. She tipped her head back and laughed in the falsest way possible.

Amber put that fake smile on her face and said, "Hey, JJ."

Her sister squealed and handed her drink to the man standing next to her. Amber saw JJ coming, saw the fake smile and sparkle in her eyes too, but she couldn't look away from that man.

He wore a cowboy hat. Blue jeans. And a simple T-shirt with a string of cartoon Christmas lights across the chest.

"You made it," JJ said, giggling obnoxiously in Amber's ear. "Come meet everyone." She took Amber's hand and led her the few feet to the group. "Hank, this is my sister. Amber, my fiancé, Hank Bell."

"I'm so glad to finally meet you," Amber said, still staring at him. She wasn't sure why she was reacting this way, only that she did not picture her sister with a cowboy. Not even a little bit.

"And his parents, Phil and Eliza," JJ said, her grip on Amber's hand tightening. Amber shook hands with everyone, getting the message loud and clear. She squeezed her sister's hand back and stepped away from her slightly.

"I didn't know you were a cowboy, Hank," she said. She'd literally never seen a single picture of him wearing any western attire.

"Oh, he's not," JJ said with a quick laugh that sounded more nervous than anything. "It was just so sunny today, and he grabbed the first hat he could find."

He obviously owned a cowboy hat to grab, but Amber didn't point that out. The mood had shifted to something awkward, and Amber turned to his parents. "Where do you guys live?"

"Alhambra," Eliza said with a smile. "And you?"

"Oh, I'm in Colorado Springs now," she said with a nod. "I grew up here and lived here for a long time. Just moved there a few months ago."

"Eliza's sister lives in the Denver area," Phil said with a smile, each word taking the awkwardness down a notch. "We love that area."

"It's beautiful," Amber said, as that had always been in her pro column.

"Didn't you have a girlfriend there once, Hank?" Phil asked, and JJ audibly sucked in a breath.

"A long time ago, Dad," Hank said easily, leaning toward JJ. "I lived in Denver for a couple of years with my aunt."

"Oh, right," JJ said, though it was clear to anyone with even one working eye that she hadn't known that. She tossed a poison-filled look to Amber, as if this conversation were her fault.

"What do you do, Hank?" she asked. "I mean, I've heard a lot about you, but I'm not sure I know what you do for a living." She smiled at him, determined to make this conversation bearable.

"I'm in agriculture," he said, and JJ cleared her throat loudly.

"Are we ready to eat, Mom?" she asked, deftly drawing Hank away from Amber and his parents.

A sigh filled Amber's body, but she didn't let it come out of her mouth.

"What are you doing in Denver?" Phil asked.

"Oh, I work for Forever Friends," Amber said, seizing onto the topic. "We're opening a new facility there. A huge ranch for rescue animals."

"Isn't there one of those around here?" Eliza asked, looking at Phil. "I think Greg got a dog from someplace like that." She glanced back at Amber. "Greg's our other son."

"Oh, great," Amber said with a smile. "And yes, Last Chance Ranch isn't too far from Alhambra. I mean, I don't know where Greg lives."

"He teaches high school in Pasadena," Eliza said. "I think the school does something with the rescue dogs there?" She looked to Amber for confirmation as memories started streaming through her mind.

The rescue dogs and the cross-country team. Lance had been responsible for that.

Hank wearing that cowboy hat. Lance wore a cowboy hat.

She continued the conversation and laughed with her family through dinner. Overall, she managed to enjoy herself, though Lance never left her mind completely.

JJ and Hank left together, followed quickly by Eliza and Phil. Amber stood at the door and waved, something moving through her that took a moment to identify.

Peace. Forgiveness. Love.

She closed the door and turned back to her parents. "What a great party," she said.

Her mother came forward and hugged her, almost the first acknowledgement of Amber that night. "It's so good to see you. Colorado is too far away."

"I know, Mom," Amber said, enjoying the warm embrace from her mother. "I know."

THE NEXT MORNING, she woke in the guest room that had used to be her bedroom on the second floor. The house felt cold, and she shivered under the blankets as she reached for her phone.

A text waited for her, and her breath stuck in her chest when she saw Adele's name on the screen.

I know you're in town for your sister's wedding. You should come out to the ranch for Christmas Eve.

The message had come late last night, after Amber had fallen into bed, exhausted. Another message sat below it.

I mean, if you can. I know you're here visiting family. But you're welcome. Christmas Eve. Six o'clock, at the homestead.

Amber read and re-read the messages. She wanted to text Adele and ask if Lance would be there, but she didn't dare. She didn't want his presence to be a deciding factor for her.

Can I call you? she typed out quickly, sending the message before she realized how early it was.

Sure. Adele's message came back almost instantly, and Amber didn't hesitate. She touched the phone icon and lifted the device to her ear.

"Hey," Adele said, fondness in her tone.

"I hope it's not too early."

"Are you kidding? James is up at the crack of dawn." Pure love rode in Adele's voice, though she was trying to make it sound like she didn't enjoy getting up with her baby.

"He's got to be so big now," Amber said, emotion choking the words as they left her throat.

"He's a monster," Adele said with a chuckle. "So, can you sneak away for Christmas Eve?"

"You know what? I think I can." She smiled as she looked out the window. No snow here, and that was a definite pro for California. "You know what I'm going to ask next."

"He'll be there," Adele said. "His mom too. And his whole family. There will be a lot of people, Amber, and you should come. We miss you, and we want to see you."

She pressed her lips together, nodding though Adele couldn't see her. "When did you know you'd made a mistake in moving to New York?"

"Oh, honey, I don't know." Adele sighed. "I loved it there, but it was a lot of work. I think I knew when I came back to the ranch and saw what I'd left behind."

"That's why you want me to come to dinner so badly."

"No," Adele said. "I think everyone has their own path." She sniffled and scuffling happened on her end of the line. "He hasn't eaten much," she said, her words not intended for Amber.

"Sorry, I was passing James off to Carson."

"It's fine," Amber said, thoughts of marriage and family right there in the forefront of her mind.

"I want you to come because I need to see you."

"You do?"

"I need to look into your face and see if you're happy in Colorado."

"And what if I'm not?"

"Then at least we'll both know."

Amber wasn't sure what Adele meant, but she knew she wanted to see her friends again. Feel the comfort and family spirit that existed at Last Chance Ranch.

"Your texts have been cryptic," Adele said. "And I just need to see you."

"I'd love to see everyone," Amber said, and that included Lance.

"Great, so you'll come."

"I'll come."

Adele exhaled like she'd just won a major victory. "Plus, Karla's pregnant, and she's dying to tell everyone." She lowered her voice as she added, "Don't tell her I told you. I'm the only one who knows, so you have to act *really* surprised."

Amber giggled, the laughter growing and growing until she and Adele were both laughing in great peals. "After that party last night," she told her friend. "I can pretend to do or be anything."

"Great, see in you a couple of days."

Chapter Twenty-Five

L ance put the final piece of tape on the presents he'd bought for his family. He didn't normally go overboard, but he'd found comfort in shopping for his loved ones this year. He piled the last gift for Tia under his tree with the others. Everyone was making the journey to the ranch for the Christmas Eve dinner at the homestead.

Scarlett had enjoyed having his mother at the ranch as she started learning how to become a mom, and Lance knew his mother had helped his boss a lot over the last several months.

He had gifts for his friends that felt like family too, and he loaded those up in a small box to take down the road and hand out before dinner. Anyone who didn't stay at Last Chance Ranch for the holidays had already emptied their stockings, and Lance had given them his gifts before they'd left for other family celebrations.

But Dave and Sissy would be there tonight, as would Sawyer and Jeri, Carson and Adele, Karla and Cache, and Scarlett and Hudson. Ames and Cook had left a couple of days ago, and Gray had quit at the ranch in October, leaving Lance as the only singleton going to the homestead that night.

Well, and his mother. And Scarlett's grandfather, but Lance didn't count them. He had come to a place in his life where he didn't feel like his relationship status mattered, which was good, because he had absolutely no inclination to change it.

He thought of Amber each day, hoping and even occasionally praying that she was happy and that Colorado held everything she wanted it to. His heart had scarred over a little bit, and he could at least enjoy the presence of his friends again without the bitter, raging jealousy tainting him.

He didn't bother knocking at the homestead, as the front door stood wide open. "I'm here," he called as he went in, automatically turning left to put his gifts in the remaining stockings that hung along the wall, over the fireplace, and around the corner toward the living room.

Scarlett came out of the kitchen, one of her boys on her hip. "Hey, Lance." She smiled at him. "Your mother just called and said Art had just arrived and they'd be over in a minute."

"Great." He finished putting the gifts in the stockings and reached for Logan. "Can I hold him?"

"You'd be doing me a favor." Scarlett passed the seven-month-old over to Lance, and the boy reached for his hat instantly.

Lance chuckled at him and leaned his head back. "Not today, bud," he said as Scarlett went back into the kitchen. Miles, the other twin, sat on the floor with a few toys scattered around him, and Lance bent to put Logan beside his brother. The child wailed instantly, and Lance picked him back up. "Oh, okay. I see how it is."

"He skipped his nap," Scarlett said from the kitchen. "He'll probably sleep through dinner and keep me up all night."

"Probably," Lance said, joining her in the kitchen. "Where's Hudson?"

"Bringing in extra chairs," she said just as the back door opened and Hudson's voice entered the house before he did. Carson came with him, and Lance lifted one hand in greeting for his two friends.

"Need more help?" he asked.

"You're helping already," Scarlett said as she stirred something on the stove. "You can't have him, Hudson. Logan's not crying."

Hudson grinned at Lance and bent over to kiss his kid. "Good boy, Logan."

Lance thought he was doing all the work, but he just smiled at the soft look on Hudson's face.

"Did you tell him, sweetheart?" Hudson asked his wife, cutting his eyes to her and back to Lance.

"No," Scarlett said, turning from her task in the kitchen. "I forgot."

"How could you forget?" Carson asked as he finished unfolding the chairs he'd brought in. He faced Lance. "I'll tell him." He drew in a deep breath, and in that short time, Lance's worries exploded.

"Amber's coming," Carson said. "Adele invited her, and she told her you'd be here, and she still said she'd come."

Lance blinked, sure the icy feeling in his chest would subside any moment. It didn't, and he'd have to figure out how to breathe through it. He was usually one breath away from falling to his knees and asking God for help as it was.

And now Amber was coming?

"Tonight?" he asked through a dry throat. In his arms, Logan started to babble, but he paid the baby no mind.

"In about an hour," Carson said.

Lance needed to sit down. He'd pictured the beautiful blonde so many times over the months she'd been gone, but he was sure a different version of the woman would arrive at the homestead, and he'd be left bleeding again.

"I'm going to put her way down on the other end of the table," Scarlett said, appearing in front of him and taking her son. She passed Logan to Hudson, but the boy fussed, trying to get back to Lance.

Lance took him again, and he immediately quieted.

"You look like we've hit you with a frying pan," Hudson said.

"It's...Amber," Lance whispered, her name so sharp on his tongue.

"He loves her," Scarlett said, turning to Hudson. "I'm going to kill Adele."

The back door opened again, and Adele entered the house with her son in her arms too. "Lance," she said as if she were surprised he was there. She stalled in the open doorway. "You told him."

"How can you tell?" Carson asked. "Is it the shocked, wide-eyed look? The way he can't breathe and blink at the same time?"

Lance was breathing and blinking, thank you very much. They were involuntary actions, after all, and that was about all he could manage to do when he allowed Amber to come this far into his mind.

"My family is coming," he said. "I can't just leave." He looked at Logan so he'd have somewhere safe to focus. He didn't want to leave. He'd been looking forward to this Christmas Eve program for weeks.

Hudson read the story of the Savior's birth from the scriptures, and Lance's soul got a dose of heavenly light he desperately needed. The food was always good, and he felt like he belonged.

But now...now, he didn't belong.

"It will be okay," Adele said, coming to stand in front

of him along with everyone else. "She's going to come back to the ranch. To you."

"You don't know that," Lance said.

"Sure I do," Adele said. "I left this place once too, when I was in love. All I needed to do was come back once." She grinned at Lance, though her eyes did hold a bit of trepidation. "I just did you a huge favor, Lance." She reached over and smoothed Logan's hair over his forehead. "You tell him, baby. She'll be back before Lance knows it." She walked into the kitchen, and Hudson and Carson ducked their heads and went back outside to get more chairs.

Scarlett alone looked at him, and Lance didn't know what to say. What to do.

"She doesn't love me," Lance said quietly. If she did, how could she have left in the first place? Why hadn't she called or texted even once? "And I don't love her. Not anymore."

"I know," Scarlett said, but her voice was false and much too high. "But we love you, Lance, and it will be okay." She hugged him then, and Lance closed his eyes, hoping she was right.

He wanted her to be right so badly. And he wanted Adele to be right too. And he knew he'd just lied, because he'd loved Amber for as long as he could remember knowing her, and there was no way he was ready to see her after only four months.

Emotion rumbled through his chest, and he stepped

away from Scarlett before she could feel it. Thankfully, his mother and brother arrived, and more kids and more people increased the noise and energy level in the homestead.

Logan laid his head against Lance's shoulder, and he hugged the boy with all the love he had. He went to greet his family, welcoming them to the homestead and introducing them around. As soon as that was finished, he said, "Amber's coming. I just found out, and I figured you guys should know."

"I knew," his mother said, and Lance's annoyance sparked to life again. "She just texted me about an hour ago," she added quickly. "I didn't have time to text you."

Lance pressed his teeth together, not wanting to be angry with anyone today. Including himself.

Kristen arrived, and he asked Sandy to let her know about Amber, and he went to find a soft spot to sit while the baby he held slept. Everyone would gather in the living room for the Christmas story before they ate anyway. Stockings would get opened. Cheer and love would be present. And then they'd eat, so he had time to sit and relax with this baby who seemed to love him when no one else did.

As soon as he thought it, he knew he'd lied to himself again. Everyone here loved him, and it wasn't fair to say they didn't.

Dave joined him on the couch, his own sleeping baby

in his arms. He also looked exhausted, and Lance just smiled at him. "How's she feeling?"

"She's getting better," Dave said. "Slowly. What about you?"

"Logan skipped his nap today."

"I meant you."

"I'm fine." He held Dave's eyes for a moment as Karla and Cache arrived, adding more chaos to the house. Scarlett had been right. Amber being here would be fine. He'd stay on his side of the room, and she could chat with all of her friends.

Carson sat between Lance and Dave, James on his lap. "I tried to tell Adele," he said.

"It will be fine," Lance said, probably harsher than he needed to. I'm an adult. So is she. We won't ruin this for anyone." Thankfully, the conversation moved to something else, and Lance only had to listen as Carson and Dave started talking about the new horses they'd gotten on the ranch in the past few weeks.

"They're completely wild," Dave said. "It's going to take a long time to break them."

"I agree," Carson said.

Lance knew the moment Amber arrived, because somehow her opening the door had caused a hush to settle on the entire ranch. He drew in a steady breath and didn't turn to look behind him. Her presence called to him, and he closed his eyes as he heard her laugh and say hello to Adele.

He hadn't laughed for weeks after she left. *Maybe she didn't either*, a voice whispered in his head, and he knew he was being unfair again. But every breath felt like work, and he felt like he was functioning with only ten-percent of his heart.

She'd taken the rest of it with her to Colorado.

"Lance." Scarlett's hand landed on the shoulder where her son wasn't sleeping.

"Yeah?"

"Amber wants to talk to you." She started to take Logan, but the boy shrieked, and she let go of him. He settled right back to silence and sleep against Lance's shoulder.

"I've got him, Scarlett," he said. "Now's not a great time to talk."

"Let's gather in the living room," Hudson said, clearly oblivious to the Amber-Lance situation. Carson couldn't seem to look away from him, but Lance just watched as the others brought in chairs or sat on the floor as they filled the living room.

Amber sat to his right, in his line of sight if he turned his head. Unfortunately, Hudson sat over there too, so that was where most people looked.

"Welcome to our home," he said, his voice low and filled with emotion. "We love each of you, and we love having you here. Our ranch family has grown so much this year." He took a few moments to look around at all the new faces and babies that were there this year.

Lance did too, and extreme gratitude for Scarlett and Hudson streamed through him. They didn't have to let his mother live here for free. They didn't have to add seven people to their Christmas table. And yet, they did, no questions asked.

Oh, how he loved them.

His eyes caught on Amber, and everything he'd ever felt for her came roaring through him. The blocks, the defenses, the scars he'd thought had healed were all broken wide open as she looked right back at him.

She tried to smile, but her chin trembled as if she might start crying. She wiped her eyes, and Lance was actually surprised. Could Adele be right? Would she feel the things he'd always felt about this place and come back?

He didn't dare to hope for such a thing, and he looked away just as his mother reached over and took Amber's hand in hers. She looked at his mom now, and his mom smiled and nodded as if they'd had more than a quick texting conversation an hour ago.

They probably had, and that used to bother Lance. Tonight, though, it didn't.

"I thought we'd go around and read a few verses each tonight," Hudson said. "Does one of the older kids want to start?" He looked at Art's kids. "Devon?"

Art handed his son his phone and pointed. Devon focused on the device and started in his clear, angelic voice, "And it came to pass in those days, that there went out a decree from...."

"Cesar Augustus," Art said quietly.

"Cesar Augustus," Devon repeated. "That all the world should be taxed."

Lance's spirit calmed, and he let himself get wrapped up in the love of the story. When it was his turn, he read, his voice steady and strong, and then he let Dave finish the story.

Silence filled the room, even with all the babies present.

"I want to be a shepherd," Hudson said. "Telling the world of the good news about the Lord. I hope I can do that by how I treat others and how I conduct business." He looked around at all of them. "I love the Lord, and I know all of you do too." He glanced at Scarlett, who smiled at him, her eyes filled with tears.

"Let's do the stockings," she said in a bright voice. "Hudson and I will pass them out." They got up to do that, and Lance leaned his head back and closed his eyes. Maybe he could just stay right here for the rest of the night.

As soon as the stockings were out, Scarlett took Logan from him, and this time the baby didn't even stir. "I'm going to go lay him down," she said, nodding to the stocking. "You get opening, Mister."

Lance cast another glance at Amber, who somehow had a stocking too. She wore a gorgeous smile to go with those brown eyes that he longed for and that gentle spirit he'd fallen for long before he'd even been out with her.

She lifted her eyes to his, and time slowed. He still managed to get the message when she nodded toward the front door, got up, and left her stocking right where it was.

Lance's gaze followed her for a moment and then looked back at his mother. She wore hope in her eyes and a smile on her face, and she motioned for Lance to go after Amber.

He barely hesitated, because he wanted to be where she was, even if it was only for tonight.

Chapter Twenty-Six

Amber swallowed, but the buzzing nerves would not be calmed.

Then Lance stepped onto the porch with her, and everything aligned. "Hey," he said. "It's...so great to see you." He took her easily into his arms, and Amber couldn't hold back the tide of tears that had been threatening to spill from her eyes since the moment she'd left her parents' house, hours ago.

She couldn't speak, so she just held onto his powerful shoulders and cried as he hugged her. To her surprise, he stepped back and wiped his eyes too, cleared his throat, and moved farther from her than she ever wanted him to be again.

"How's Denver?" he asked, his voice gruff but steady.

"You know what?" she asked. "It's terrible. I hate it there."

He looked at her, and all the texts Amber had wanted to send to him over the months sprang into her mind. "I'm so sorry," she whispered. "Is there any way we could try again?"

A frown furrowed his brows. "I don't see how, Amber. You live somewhere else, and I can barely manage an in-person relationship."

Amber moved closer to him, keeping a respectable distance between them. It felt like a gulf she couldn't get across by herself.

Of course she couldn't. She couldn't do anything by herself. But she could take one step—a leap of faith—and hope the Lord would build a bridge as she continued to walk.

"You're the best boyfriend I've ever had," she said, not sure where the words came from. "I made a mistake. Or maybe I didn't. I felt so right about going to Denver. But... I'm not happy there."

Feeling reckless and brave at the same time, she reached over and touched his hand. When he didn't flinch away, she curled her fingers around his. "I want to come back. I want to come *home*."

He looked at her, those bright blue eyes firing over and over.

"I've never said this to anyone." She swallowed again, but the words wouldn't budge. "I love you, Lance Long-comb. And maybe God sent me to Colorado so I would realize it. I don't know. I just know I'm going to do whatever I can to come back to this ranch, because there's nowhere like this place anywhere else on Earth."

Several seconds of silence passed, and then he asked, "This is about me, right? Not my mother. Not your friends."

Amber turned toward him, a true smile lighting her soul. "Lance, this is *all* about you. I'm miserable without you, and I'm honestly dumbfounded how I thought I could survive without you. I want you to be *my* cowboy. I want a cowboy Christmas every year—with you. I—"

He stole her next sentence from her by kissing her, his mouth hard at first. Unyielding. Taking. Searching.

He kissed her roughly for a moment, softening after that, and testifying to her that he hadn't forgotten about her. Hadn't gotten over her. "I love you, too," he whispered against her lips, quickly joining their mouths again.

Whatever Amber had thought their reunion would be like, it wasn't this. There were so many details to work out. When she pulled away and said that, Lance said, "They're just details. If I know you want to be with me, we can get all the little stuff lined up."

"I want to be with you."

Lance nodded and gazed across the street again, tucking her right against his side. "I miss you so much," he whispered.

"I've written you dozens of texts," she said just as quietly. "I keep them in a folder on my phone instead of sending them." Tears choked her again, and Lance's arm tightened around her.

"Guys," Adele said from behind them. "We're getting ready to eat."

Amber turned and found questions in her friend's eyes. "All right. We're coming." She stepped away from Lance, but he caught her hand as she went. Adele saw it, a smile filling her face as she too ducked back into the house.

"Amber," Lance said, and she stopped and twisted back to him.

He searched her face, so many emotions storming across his. "I'll do everything I can to make you happy again."

"Is it that obvious that I'm not happy?"

"To me it is."

"I don't have a gypsy spirit," she whispered.

He smiled and leaned down to touch his nose to hers. "Yes, you do, sweetheart. But even gypsies can fall in love and build a life in one place."

"That's what I want," she said, and she hadn't even known it until the possibility wasn't there anymore. God had taken her to Colorado, but it wasn't for the reasons Amber had thought it was. Not even close.

"Seeing you with that baby was pretty sexy," she said playfully as they entered the homestead together.

"Oh, you liked that, did you?" He grinned at her and paused to close the door behind them. "Let's get married quick, sweetheart. Then we can have our own babies that I'll hold while they sleep."

Amber pressed against the fear threatening to overtake her. "I'd like that, Lance."

"Yeah?" He chuckled and touched his lips to her forehead. "I thought it would take a bit more convincing. Can't change your mind on that one, you know."

His words stung, but Amber understood where he was coming from. She did seem to change her mind on a whim. Take new jobs. Flit from boyfriend to boyfriend. Move across state lines.

They just needed more time together to build their relationship back to what it had been before she'd left. In fact, Amber knew their relationship would never be what it was before she'd left.

It would be better, because she was better than she'd been a year ago.

"Oh, you two made up." Jamie Lee rushed toward them, tears streaming down her face. "I knew you would. You two are made for each other."

She hugged them both, Lance saying, "Mom, you're embarrassing me again," before he laughed into his mother's shoulder.

Amber couldn't laugh, because she knew Jamie Lee was absolutely right. *Thank you for showing me how perfect Lance is for me*, she prayed as the embrace broke up and Adele called to them again to come and eat.

"First," Karla said, stepping in front of the line. "Cache and I have an announcement."

Amber started crying again as Scarlett said, "Shut the front door. Karla?"

"We're going to have a baby this summer." Karla's joy shone for the world to see, just the way the new star had on the night of the Savior's birth.

The whole house erupted into cheers and congratulations, and Lance pulled Amber closer, his lips against her earlobe as he said, "I love you," one more time.

———

"She said that?" Lance asked, looking at Amber for longer than was comfortable, though no one was on the road this early in the morning.

"From her lips," Amber said. "She said I could not get engaged until she was married, because it would 'divide my mom's attention.'"

Lance shook his head and finally looked back out the windshield. "Unbelievable."

"They'll all be on their best behavior today," Amber said, snuggling into his side. "So it's the perfect day to meet them." She shouldn't be so nervous to bring him to meet her family, but she barely wanted to be there so she couldn't fathom why Lance would want to come with her to her sister's wedding.

But he said he did, and they'd just gotten back

together a couple of days ago, and Amber wanted to be with him as much as possible before she had to board a plane and fly back to Denver.

She'd spent most of yesterday on the phone with Jewel, and they had a meeting the following day that had Amber's heart in knots already.

Lance eventually pulled up to the event center that JJ loved and pulled into a spot next to her father's car. He didn't get out, and neither did Amber.

She finally released her breath and asked, "Ready?"

"So ready," he said, taking off his hat and straightening it as he put it back on.

"Oh, another thing," Amber said. "JJ has insisted her fiancée isn't a cowboy, but when I finally met him a few days ago, he was wearing a cowboy hat."

"She doesn't like cowboys or something?"

"Oh, no," Amber said, meeting his eyes.

He looked terrified. "I'm a cowboy."

"And I love cowboys." She grinned at him. "And you're way better than her almost-husband, and she's not going to like you."

"Great," he grumbled. "Your mom and dad?"

"They'll love you," she said, nudging him to get out of the truck. "Now let's go."

Lance got out of the truck and re-tucked his shirt. He wore a dark pair of black slacks with a matching shirt, with a tie the color of the cranberries they'd had on Christmas Eve. His dress hat was also black, and she fully expected someone to ask him if he thought he was at a funeral. She just hoped it wasn't someone in her family.

He turned back to her and helped her down from the truck so she could also straighten her skirt. She wore a silver dress that glittered in the sunlight, with a pair of bright blue pumps that brought her closer to Lance's height.

She slipped her hand into his and they faced the doors together. Before she got there, her father came outside, a smile on his face.

"Hey, sweetie." He drew her into a hug and then glanced at Lance.

"Dad," Amber said. "This is my boyfriend, Lance Longcomb."

"The Lance you were dating over the summer?"

"Yes, sir," Lance said, reaching out to shake her father's hand. "It's so great to meet you." He wore a brilliant smile, and Amber watched her father melt right in front of her eyes.

"We got back together," she said by way of explanation. "And I volunteered him to help set up." She opened the door her father had just come out. "So let's go, Lance."

"You didn't see me," her father muttered. "Mom's on a rampage."

"So should we wait?" Amber said, pausing before going in.

"Maybe," her dad said. "Apparently the florist isn't

here yet, and if we don't have the flowers in the next ten minutes everything will be ruined."

Amber exchanged a glance with Lance, and he shrugged. "Let's just get it over with," Amber said, continuing inside.

"I don't care about flowers, by the way," he said, his lips right at her ear again. A shiver spiraled down her spine.

"No?" she said. "What if the roses are pink instead of red? Will you die?"

"If you showed up, I'd die of happiness." He chuckled, and they rounded a corner to find her mom almost yelling into her cell phone.

Amber let her finish, and then she said, "Here goes nothing." She moved forward on strong legs and said, "Mom, this is Lance."

She looked him up and down, her eyes appraising every inch of clothing, the hat, the grin on his face. She finally softened and smiled too.

"Lovely to meet you," Lance said, and Amber almost started laughing. "We just heard about the flowers from your husband. How can I help?"

"Oh, the...." She shook his hand, clearly unable to talk and shake at the same time. "If someone could get what she has ready, we could at least get the dining hall ready."

"Text me an address," Lance said to Amber as he started backing away.

"You're going?" she asked.

"Sure," he said easily. "I'll be back before you know it, and you guys can keep working here." He came back toward her and swept one arm around her, leaning down to kiss her quickly. He kept his mouth at her ear and said, "You're amazing. Don't let them make you think you're not."

Then he was gone. Amber stared after him, trying to remember how to do more than one thing at a time.

"He's...."

"Wonderful," Amber supplied. "Perfect for me." She sighed, and her mother laced her arm through Amber's.

"Is there another wedding on the horizon?"

"There better be," Amber said, turning into her mom and laughing. Her mother relaxed after that, and they went back into the dining hall to see what else needed to be done.

Amber couldn't wait until Lance returned, because then she could show him off to everyone.

Chapter Twenty-Seven

Lance sat next to Amber at the wedding, his own nerves about to launch him out of the seat. The man her sister had hired to marry them had about as much enthusiasm as a potato, and Lance had nodded off at least three times.

Then he'd remember what he had in his pocket, and his adrenaline would roar back to life.

Amber couldn't get engaged until JJ got married. No problem. She'd be married any minute now, if the preacher would get to the point of this shindig. Then Lance could ask Amber to be his wife, and they could start planning their lives together.

She had a meeting with her boss tomorrow, and he didn't think it would go well. Amber had assured him that she would be coming back to California whether she had a job or not, but he really didn't want it to come to that.

"I do," Hank finally said, and the preacher said they were man and wife. A cheer went up as they kissed, and Amber stood, her clapping quite loud as she applauded.

Lance joined her, seeing the happiness and love she had for her sister, even if JJ annoyed her. Forgot about her. Snubbed her.

He'd been right about one thing—Amber was not the same woman he'd wooed with doughnuts last year. She was just as beautiful, sure. Just as kind. Just as hard-working.

But she had more depth now. She'd matured, and Lance could barely contain his excitement over the diamond in his pocket.

He couldn't get her alone until after the dinner. After the dancing. After the event center had been cleared, and they got back in the truck. They were staying at her parents' house that night, and Lance wanted her to be his fiancée before they got there.

She exhaled, a long, slow hiss coming from her mouth.

"That was actually fun," he said. "Except for that pastor. He was a snoozefest."

Amber snorted and then started laughing. "He was, wasn't he?"

Lance shook his head. "Sorry, that was probably rude."

"We're getting married by Pastor Williams," she said. "At the ranch. With all the dogs on the side of the road."

"Oh, we are, huh?" He looked at her, and with only

the light shining from the streetlights, she was soft and beautiful. "When might you want to do that?"

"I don't know," she said. "You haven't even asked me yet."

He reached into his pocket and took out the diamond, pinching it between his forefinger and his thumb until she realized what he held.

"Lance," she gasped, covering her mouth with both hands.

"I'm in love with you," he said, his emotions choosing now to infect his voice. He didn't care. He just kept going. "I've loved you for years, and while I didn't quite have the faith that you'd come back to me, you did. You proved me wrong, and I hope you'll surprise me for the rest of our lives."

Tears filled her eyes, and she didn't even try to wipe them away as they fell.

"Will you marry me?"

She nodded immediately, and he blinked back his own tears as he slid the ring on her left hand. She took his face in both of her hands and kissed him, a slow, sensual kiss that told him how much she loved him.

But it was still nice to hear when she said, "I love you, Lance."

"And I love you, Amber. Let's go show your parents and get a date on the calendar."

"THAT GOES IN THE KITCHEN," Amber said from her spot on her new front porch. Lance grinned at her as he passed with the box he'd unloaded from her truck. He'd flown to Denver and driven the beast back when he'd heard about the flat tire she'd encountered on the way there.

Not only that, but he could see her front porch from his, and he couldn't wait until March, when they would have a shared front porch.

A shared cabin. A shared bed.

He dropped the box on the kitchen counter and turned to go get something else. Hudson and Carson came in carrying a couch, and Lance stood out of the way as they maneuvered it into place.

Amber had left Forever Friends on good terms. Her terms. Scarlett had hired her as a goat trainer and yoga instructor, a program that wasn't funded by the non-profit that gave the ranch a lot of money.

Not only that, but she'd approached the local fitness center about starting curvy women aerobics classes, and they'd jumped at the idea. Her first one was tomorrow, and she'd shown them a routine via video from her apartment in Colorado.

"Women carrying extra pounds should feel beautiful," she'd told him. "The way you make me feel beautiful."

"You are beautiful," he'd told her, and then she'd explained how sometimes bigger people wanted their own space to exercise in.

"And they agreed. I got the job." She'd been thrilled, and Lance was happy about whatever made her happy.

Hours later, with all of her belongings off the truck and in the cabin, they sat on the front steps, their hands intertwined.

"Thank you," she said, leaning her head against his bicep. "For everything, Lance. Really. Thank you."

He laid his cheek against her head. He'd said everything he needed to say. There wasn't a conversation they hadn't had that they needed to. So he just said, "I love you," and she said it back.

This woman at his side and those words coming from her mouth created joy for him, and Lance couldn't ask for more than that.

He did, however, send up his own prayer of gratitude to the Lord for all the love and support he'd received in those few dark months while Amber hadn't been in his life.

Thank You, God, he thought.

"Praise the Lord," he whispered, and she said, "Yes. He deserves all the thanks and glory, doesn't He?"

Yes, He did.

"What will you wear at our wedding?" he asked.

She sighed happily at his side. "I've actually found the perfect dress...."

Read on for a sneak peek at RHETT'S MAKE-BELIEVE MARRIAGE, where you'll get great cowboy billionaire romance, Christmas romance, fake marriages, and heartwarming family saga across all 7 books - all available now!

Sneak Peek! RHETT'S MAKE-BELIEVE MARRIAGE
Chapter One

"I t's totally fine," Evelyn Foster said to the woman on the other end of the line. "Not every first date goes well." She often had to counsel her clients through a few dates before they could see what she saw.

Being a small-town matchmaker, where ninety percent of the men were cowboys, wasn't an easy job. But Evelyn loved it, as she could make everything line up on paper like a dream. The women knew what she was doing, but the men...well, sometimes men just needed to get out of their own way.

And Evelyn provided a way for them to do that—and conveniently run into the woman of their dreams. They just didn't know it yet.

And obviously, Tina didn't know it yet either. "He's perfect for you," Evelyn assured her. "What happened that rubbed you the wrong way?"

"For starters, he wanted to take me to the big box store for a date."

Evelyn could hear the eyeroll in Tina's voice.

"But you persuaded him to do something else, right?" Evelyn asked, shuffling a couple of pages on the desk in front of her. The wind shook the windows of her office, and she glanced outside to see a dust storm had kicked up on the farm where she lived with her sisters.

Granted, they didn't really use the two hundred acres they had, as that was a lot for three women to manage by themselves. Their father had retired a few years ago, and they mostly planted as much as they could and sold the hay to other farms and ranches surrounding Three Rivers.

"I did, yes," Tina said. "But is that going to be my whole life moving forward? Me trying to persuade this guy to do what I want?"

"Let me look through a few more candidates," Evelyn said, focusing on her papers again. May was an exceptionally busy time for her services, as well as around the Shining Star Ranch. While her oldest sister, Callie, ran most of what happened on the ranch, Evelyn had plenty of chores to do too. "And I'll get back to you in a couple of days, okay?"

"Okay," Tina said. "What should I do if Gideon calls?"

"You get to decide that," Evelyn said, looking at Gideon's one-sheet. "He really does seem perfect for you.

Maybe he just didn't want to commit to something as long as dinner."

"I don't know how that's a plus," Tina said dryly.

"Well, he's met you once, for what? Five minutes at the dry cleaner? Somewhere I only knew he'd be because we got a last-minute phone call." Evelyn never revealed her sources, but she had spies all over the town of Three Rivers.

With a population of almost seventeen thousand now, she certainly couldn't be everywhere at once, or know where every eligible bachelor would be at any given time.

"And that was the first time he'd been there," Evelyn reminded her. "So maybe give him a little slack?" She spoke as kindly as she could. After all, Tina was paying her, and she didn't need to lose a client because the cowboy Tina had her eye on was out of his element.

"Okay." Tina sighed. "But still look at a couple of other guys for me."

"Anyone in mind?" Evelyn asked, because no one else on her list stood out for someone like Tina. She liked a through-and-through Texas cowboy, with a big hat, and the biggest belt buckle possible. Rodeo experience a plus.

While there were plenty of cowboys in Three Rivers, Tina wanted Cowboy Extreme.

"I've seen a man at church the last few weeks," Tina said. "He looks new in town."

Evelyn repressed a sigh and looked out the window again. She couldn't see the trees she knew were only ten feet away. Alarms started sounding in her mind, and surprise darted through her that she hadn't lost cell phone reception yet.

"I don't know his name or where he lives," Tina said.

"All right," Evelyn said. "I'll put out some feelers to find out who this guy is." With that, the line crackled, and Tina's words broke up. In the next moment, the service cut out, and Evelyn looked at her phone to see the call had indeed been severed.

"Great," she muttered. Now she had to hunt down a mystery cowboy who was new to town. Maybe Patrick would know. Her boyfriend worked the meat counter at the grocery store, and he saw a lot of people—especially single cowboys coming to buy their steak dinners.

Of course, a lot of the cowboys around Three Rivers worked on farms and ranches, and they often got plenty of beef for free from their employers. So maybe Patrick wouldn't know. But it couldn't hurt to ask him.

He knew what Evelyn did for a living, and he often sent her texts with information on men she needed to know about. She couldn't send him a text right then, as it seemed her provider had gone down with the crazy windstorm.

She left her office at the same time a horrible, glass-shattering sound filled the whole farmhouse. She screamed, hers matching her younger sister's in the living room.

Callie burst in the back door with the words, "There's

a tornado headed this way. Come help me with the animals." She spun away before either Evelyn or Simone could answer.

Thankfully, Evelyn already had shoes on, and she hurried after her oldest sister, saying, "The sirens haven't even gone off. Maybe it's just a windstorm."

The moment she finished speaking, the chilling, distinct wail of the tornado siren filled the air.

She ran after Callie, who handed her a grease pen and a handful of fly masks. "Put our phone number on their sides. Put on the fly mask, and we'll set them in the pasture."

They didn't have the hurricane clips or reinforced beams needed to tether the horses securely in the barn, and their horses were used to roaming in pastures.

"Maybe it'll go north," Callie said, her voice panicked. "Like that last one."

The last tornado had been over two years ago, and it had indeed turned north before inflicting too much damage on Three Rivers. She handed Simone the same items she had Evelyn, and the sisters got to work.

"We have to go next door, too," Callie said. "We'll put our number on the animals at Fox Hill for the new owner."

"Who is it?" Evelyn asked, glancing east though she couldn't see more than five feet in either direction. Even Callie's voice coming through the swirling dirt and dust felt eerie and otherworldly.

"Some guy," Callie said vaguely, which meant she

didn't know either. "Last name's Walker, I think. Mason texted a couple of days ago and said he'd be here this week, and that we could turn the keys over to him then."

Mason Martin had lived and cultivated Fox Hill Ranch next door for years and years before deciding to up and move to Hawaii, of all places. He'd put the ranch up for sale, and contracted with the sisters to take care of the few animals he'd left behind. He had a staff of four still on the premises too, and Evelyn wondered why they couldn't take care of their own horses.

"What about Orion?" she asked. "Can't he turn the horses out to pasture over there?" It was at least a half-mile to Fox Hill, though their properties touched one another along a fence line on the east side of the ranch. Evelyn did *not* want to get caught out in the storm.

"They went into town this morning," Callie said, finishing with her last horse, smacking it on the flank and saying, "Go on. Stay safe."

With their own livestock numbered and protected as much as possible, the three sisters piled into Callie's pickup truck and rumbled down the road. If anything, the wind blew stronger at Fox Hill, but Evelyn kept her head down and her fingers moving as she marked the eight horses Mason had left behind.

He also had two pigs, six goats, and a whole herd of chickens. The tornado would likely pick them up and carry them off, and she certainly didn't know how to hold one long enough to write a phone number on feathers.

With all the animals marked that could be, Callie shouted, "We have to go inside!"

Exactly what Evelyn didn't want to do, at least not here. But one look at the sky, and she knew she didn't have a choice. Panic filled her, though she'd lived through tornadoes before. They weren't super common in this area of Texas, but she'd had enough experience with them to know what to do in case of an emergency.

"Where's Daddy?" Simone asked.

"He's with Granny," Callie yelled, holding her hat on her head as she ran for the back door of Mason's homestead.

It felt strangely quiet inside, with the three of them panting as they sucked at air that finally wasn't filled with debris.

"Come on," Callie said. "He'll have a tornado shelter."

Evelyn had been to Mason's house several times, and she knew right where it was. As Callie turned to go down a hallway, she said, "It's over here, guys. He showed it to me once." She hated that she wasn't in her own home, protecting it and herself.

But just inside the living room off the front door, she swept aside the rug and pointed to the hatch door there. "Goes down into a cement foundation."

"Get in," Callie said as glass broke somewhere in the house. The tornado might not strike Three Rivers directly, but this wind was definitely wicked and causing some real damage.

Evelyn went first and turned on her phone's flashlight. Callie followed and did the same, with Simone bringing up the rear. No sooner had Simone closed the door above them and come down the steps did it open again.

Callie shone her flashlight on the man sliding down the steps, pure fear in every line on his face. "Who are you?" she asked as Evelyn swung her light onto him too.

He bore a strong jaw and dark eyes—exactly the kind of man Evelyn would be interested in. You know, if she wasn't already dating someone.

The stranger drew in a deep breath and spoke in an even deeper voice. "I'm Rhett Walker. This is my ranch." He dusted himself off with a pair of big hands and added, "You must be the Foster sisters from next door."

"Guilty," Callie said, lowering her light so it wasn't shining right in Rhett's face. But Evelyn couldn't do the same. His good looks and bass voice seemed to have frozen her to the spot, and all she could do was stare while her heart pounded wildly in her chest.

"Can you stop shining that in my face?" he asked, his voice a touch colder than before, and Callie put her hand on Evelyn's arm to make her put the phone down.

"So," he said with only the soft glow on his features now. He was somehow sexier and more beautiful than in the harsh light, and Evelyn wondered where in the world all these thoughts and feelings were coming from. "I guess the tornado is welcoming me to the Texas Panhandle." He laughed, and Simone and Callie joined him.

Evelyn simply reveled in the sound of his laughter, thinking that if she weren't with Patrick, she'd definitely be setting herself up with one cowboy Rhett Walker.

Callie started to detail what they'd done for his animals and why they'd come in his house instead of theirs, and Evelyn shied behind her sister so she could continue to simply stare at her new next-door neighbor.

Sneak Peek! RHETT'S MAKE-BELIEVE MARRIAGE
Chapter Two

R hett Walker could not believe his rotten luck. It seemed like he'd run into a string of it, and he wondered when it would end. Just like this blasted tornado. It seemed to go on for a long time, and not only because he was trapped in his own storm shelter with three strangers.

Women, sure, but they chatted more with each other than him. He'd switched on the flashlight on his phone and currently stood in front of a long shelf with dozens of cans on it. At least they wouldn't starve down here.

"How do you know when the tornado is over?" he asked, thinking he needed a camera that showed the weather outside so he wouldn't have to risk losing his hat to check. He felt six eyes on him, but when he turned, only one woman still stared at him.

"Evelyn, right?" he asked, taking a step closer to her.

"Right," she said, her voice hoarse. She coughed, and Rhett watched her. "Sorry," she added. "We were out in the dust and dirt for a while before coming in." She cleared her throat and bent down to a lower shelf.

She straightened and held two bottles of water in her hand. "Do you mind if I have one of these?" She extended the second one toward him, and he took it.

"No problem."

"Where are you from? Have you been in a lot of tornadoes?"

"I grew up outside of Austin?" Why he phrased it like a question, he wasn't sure. He found himself clearing his own throat, as if this woman made him nervous. Everything about coming out to a ranch made him squirm a little, and three of his brothers were supposed to be with him. But there had been some problems at the office a couple of days ago, and he'd ended up coming north himself.

"I know where Austin is," Evelyn said with a small smile. She hid it behind the water bottle as she drank.

Of course she did, and suddenly the storm shelter felt a little too hot. He returned his attention to the shelves in front of him. "My father owned a technology company there," he said, glancing at her. "This shelter needs one of his cameras, then we'd know when the tornado has passed."

"You'll be able to tell," she said. "Even without a camera."

"You think so?" He wasn't sure how, as it wasn't like there were any windows in the shelter.

"A camera would get knocked around in a storm," she said, cocking her head at him, the questions clear.

Rhett shuffled his feet, but he kept his eyes on hers. "My dad had contracts with the military and government," he said. "The cameras were tiny."

"Tiny? How tiny?"

"Pinhead tiny," he said. "The wind wouldn't knock it off." As if the world had been holding its breath and had just released it, something changed. He looked up to the ceiling, the lack of groaning evident. "I think the storm is over."

"It's passing," one of Evelyn's sisters said, and Rhett couldn't believe that she could tell without visual proof. "Let's give it a few more minutes," the other woman said.

"Callie," Evelyn said, providing Rhett with the name he'd forgotten, though they'd only been in the shelter for maybe ten minutes. "She's the oldest," she added in a mock whisper, and Rhett got the message.

A chuckle started in the back of his throat, and he ducked his head as he tried to quiet it. "A little bossy, is that what you're saying?"

"She has moments," Evelyn said, and Rhett met her eyes again. She had a beautiful smile to go with that long, dark hair and those sparkling eyes. He couldn't really tell what color those were in the glow of flashlights, and he told his heart to stop skipping beats.

He hadn't bought this ranch out in the middle of nowhere to get his heart broken again. He'd managed to do that in Austin, thank you very much.

"I'm the oldest," Rhett said. "Six younger brothers."

"Wow," Evelyn said, those eyes still shining at him. "I thought some of them were coming with you."

"They are," he said. "The twins got held up in Austin, tying up loose ends, but I had to come up for the job."

She cocked her head again. "The ranch is fine."

"Oh, Jeremiah is going to mostly be doing the ranch stuff," he said. "I'll help a little. The twins are technology dudes, but they insisted on coming." He shrugged, because Tripp and Liam didn't even own plaid shirts.

"So what's the job?" she asked.

"I'm a forensic veterinarian," he said. "There's a case up here that's expected to take a while. My dad's company was selling, and this place was for sale...." He let the words hang there.

Evelyn's eyes narrowed. "Have you ever lived on a ranch?"

Before he had to answer that, Callie said, "I'm going up." That caused movement, and while Evelyn watched him for an extra moment, she too moved toward the ladder. He let them all go up first, feeling like perhaps he should've done so to make sure no one got hurt.

Thankfully, the house still stood at the top of the ladder, though there were several windows broken.

"Looks bad," Callie said, walking over the dirt that had been blown in through the broken windows.

"This is bad?" Rhett asked, not quite the house and ranch tour he'd been expecting. The weight of the clean-up felt like tons and tons, and he couldn't shoulder it. He stood in the middle of the kitchen, turning slowly.

The appliances were still there. Countertops. Even the kitchen table and barstools.

The women had gone out the back door, and Rhett went out onto the deck as well. He had so many questions, and he'd been hoping he could ask the four men who supposedly lived here on this ranch he'd bought.

Only Evelyn paused at the edge of the lawn and lifted her hand in a friendly wave, and Rhett returned it. Then she turned and followed her sisters, their red pickup firing up and rumbling down the road to the west, where their ranch obviously was.

He sighed and looked up into the still angry sky. "Really, Lord? A tornado? What am I supposed to do now?"

He had the very strong feeling that he better get to work, so he went into the garage and found a broom. After all, God had led him here, and he couldn't leave now.

Rhett had most of the main floor swept out when his phone rang. "Hello?" He didn't recognize the number, but he had a feeling he'd be answering a lot of calls from people he didn't know in the near future.

"Mister Walker?" a cowboy drawled.

"Yep, you got 'im," he said.

"I'm Orion Goldberg," the other cowboy said. "We got stuck in town and wondered where you ended up during the tornado. Maybe you're not in town yet?"

"I'm at Fox Hill," he said, pushing the huge pile of dirt out onto the deck. Everywhere he looked, there was more work to do, as evidenced by the patio table and chairs his eyes caught on. The umbrella was still there, but bent, and a sigh passed through his whole soul.

"Arrived just before the tornado. Good news," he said, trying to find the silver lining in this situation, the way his mother had always done. "The storm shelter is stocked with food and fits four people." With room for more.

"Four people?"

"The women from down the road were here," Rhett said, thinking immediately of Evelyn. He consciously switched his thoughts to how he needed to rename the ranch now that he'd finally arrived.

Just another thing in a long to-do list.

"Well, we're still in Three Rivers," Orion said, his voice fading for a moment. "What do you need us to bring back? How'd the windows fare? The animals?"

Jeremiah was supposed to be here to run the ranch, and Rhett had paid little attention to the type and number of animals on the ranch.

"Uh...." He looked out over the land behind the homestead and found several outbuildings. Barns and stables and coops. He turned away from them, overwhelmed and thankful for the four men who would be back soon. Hopefully. "There are several broken windows. Dirt and stuff everywhere. I'm sweeping out the house now."

"We'll bring back lumber and some cleaning supplies. What about groceries?"

"Can I call something in?" Rhett asked, turning back to the house. He'd bought the ranch a couple of months ago, but he and his brothers hadn't made the move immediately. The owner had said his neighbors and the crew at Fox Hill could manage for a while, and they obviously had.

"To where?" Orion asked, and that answered Rhett's question. It only took fifteen minutes to drive into the town of Three Rivers, and it was a bustling place. At least Mason Martin had told him it was. Rhett had come straight to the ranch when he'd seen the windstorm kick up and the sky turn an ugly shade of green.

"Never mind," he said.

"We can bring out some food, boss," Orion said, and Rhett wasn't used to being the boss. He worked for the state as a forensic veterinarian, and while there were only a few people who did what he did, he wasn't the boss.

"That would be great," he said. If they wanted him to be the boss, he could do it. "I'll pay you back." He outlined a few grocery staples for Orion, and the call ended. As he

0

swept the dirt back onto the ground where it belonged, he supposed things at Fox Hill could be worse. He could be the only one here, with no money to pay for anything.

As it was, he had a crew coming back with the supplies he needed, and his brothers on their way. Oh, and plenty of money, as when his father had sold the company he'd built, he'd gotten billions for it.

All the Walker brothers now had billions too—which was how Rhett had gotten this ranch in the first place. It was the second-biggest one in the area, and well-maintained. At least it had been.

"And it will be again," Rhett vowed. "But it needs a new name. A fresh start." Just like him and his brothers.

"So what do we call it?" he mused aloud to himself, not quite used to so much country stillness and silence. He and three of his brothers would be living here. "Four...." The only word he could think of was men, and that sounded stupid.

Plus, once Wyatt finished with the rodeo circuit, he'd probably come to the ranch too. With Rhett's parents retired and living in Grand Cayman now, there was no "home" for the rodeo king to return to.

"Seven Sons," Rhett said, the name popping into his head. It fit. It was perfect, and while Rhett certainly hadn't appreciated all of the rotten luck that had brought him to this part of Texas, he tipped his head back and looked up into the clearing sky.

"Thank you, Lord," he whispered, because he at least

had a place to stay, money to fund the rebuilding of this place, and family coming.

He didn't need a wife, despite what his mother said. Oh, no, he did not.

Read this family saga romance with a brand-new family of cowboy billionaires and fun family traditions on an amazing Texas ranch!

Scan the QR code for a direct link to Rhett's Make-Believe Marriage in paperback.

Seven Sons Ranch in Three Rivers Romance Series

Meet the cowboy billionaire brothers at Seven Sons Ranch. The Walkers are new in Three Rivers, and they've got the women circling. Every contemporary romance in this series features a fake marriage that turns to more, family holiday traditions, and the family saga that will create a space for you in the Walker family too!

Rhett's Make-Believe Marriage (Book 1): To save her business, she'll have to risk her heart. She needs a husband to be credible as a matchmaker. He wants to help a neighbor. **Will their fake marriage take them out of the friend zone?**

Last Chance Ranch Romance series

Journey to Last Chance Ranch and meet curvy, mature women looking for love later in life. Experience sisterhood, goat yoga, and a fake marriage against a stunning, inspirational ranch background—and some sexy cowboys too— from USA Today bestseller and Top 10 Kindle All-Star author Liz Isaacson!

Last Chance Ranch (Book 1): A cowgirl down on her luck hires a man who's good with horses and under the hood of a car. Can Hudson fine tune Scarlett's heart as they work together? Or will things backfire and make everything worse at Last Chance Ranch?

About Liz

Liz Isaacson writes inspirational romance, usually set in Texas, or Montana, or anywhere else horses and cowboys exist. She lives in Utah, where she walks her dogs daily, watches a lot of Netflix, and eats a lot of peanut butter M&Ms while writing. Find her on her website at feelgood-fictionbooks.com.

AFTER THE REVELATION

Brian Stableford's scholarly work includes *New Atlantis: A Narrative History of Scientific Romance* (Wildside Press, 2016), *The Plurality of Imaginary Worlds: The Evolution of French roman scientifique* (Black Coat Press, 2017) and *Tales of Enchantment and Disenchantment: A History of Faerie* (Black Coat Press, 2019). He has translated more than three hundred volumes from the French, mostly in the genres of *roman scientifique, contes de fées* and Romantic and Symbolist fiction.

His recent fiction includes the visionary science fiction novel *The Revelations of Time and Space* (2020) and its sequel *After the Revelation* (2021); the last in his long series of "Tales of the Genetic Revolution," *The Elusive Shadows* (2020); and the comedy fantasy *Meat on the Bone* (2021), all published by Snuggly Books.

SNUGGLY BOOKS